FLOUR BABIES

ANNE FINE

Resource Material
Rachel O'Neill

Series Consultant
Cecily O'Neill

Collins Educational
An Imprint of HarperCollins*Publishers*

Published by Collins Educational
77-85 Fulham Palace Road, London W6 8JB
An imprint of HarperCollins *Publishers*

www.CollinsEducation.com
On-line support for schools and colleges

First published in 1996

Reprinted 1997, 1998, 2000 **(twice)**

The novel *Flour Babies* was first published by Hamish Hamilton in
1992. It is available in Puffin.

ISBN 000 330312 8

Acknowledgements
The following permissions to reproduce material are gratefully
acknowledged:

Illustrations: Telegraph Colour Library pp 73, 74. The Movie Store
Collection p 79. Innes Studios p 84.

Text extracts: From *Gregory's Girl* by Bill Forsyth, Stanley Thornes
Ltd pp 60–63; from *Saved* by Edward Bond, Eyre Methuen pp 67–69;
from *My Dear Son* © Fergal Keane pp 72–73; *The Child* by Michael
Roberts, Faber and Faber Ltd p 75; from *Flour Babies* (the novel) by
Anne Fine, Penguin Books Ltd pp 82–83; from *It was just too much
too young* by Lisa O'Kelly, The Observer pp 85–87. Please note:
whilst every effort has been made to contact owners of copyright
material, this has not been possible in every case.

Design by Wendi Watson
Cover design by Chi Leung
Cover photograph by Mark Kensett, Innes Studios

Commissioning Editor: Domenica de Rosa
Editors: Helen Clark, Katie Anderson
Production: Susan Cashin

Typeset by Harper Phototypesetters Ltd, Northampton
Printed in China

CONTENTS

BACKGROUND TO THE PLAY

The idea for *Flour Babies* was just about handed to me on a plate. As I came out of Boots the Chemist one day, someone pressed on me a copy of *Awake!*, the Jehovah's Witnesses' newsletter. In it, I found an amusing snippet about a Californian High School in which the teenage pregnancy rate had shot up so high that, in desperation, a project was begun. Each pupil was given a six-pound sack of flour to care for over three weeks. These 'flour babies' had to be kept dry, clean and safe at all times. If the owner went out, a responsible babysitter had to be found, and each pupil had to keep a diary. At the end of the three weeks, a typical pupil's commentary was: 'I was **amazed**. It didn't scream. It couldn't crawl. I didn't have to feed it, and it didn't mess its diapers. And **still** I couldn't wait to be rid of it.' (Almost needless to say, the number of teenage pregnancies in this school suddenly plummeted.)

The book clearly had to be curtailed in a few ways, to make a play. At an obvious level, I've had to kill off a good few of Simon's classmates, so as not to clutter up the stage. Mr Cartright's sheer cynicism about school projects (which I'll openly admit I share) comes over more strongly in the novel. Also, some of the comedy culled from Dena Attar's delicious polemic on the teaching of social and domestic subjects in schools (*Wasting Girls' Time*, Virago, 1990) didn't make it from the pages of the novel to the play. But there's enough left to show the differing ways in which the pupils respond to the traumas of the experiment.

A natural question might be: why set the story in a boys' school? I'm afraid this is a stab at realism. I suspect it's all too likely that, in any mixed group, some soft female soul (and it only takes one) would crack and offer to look after all the flour babies. You might take issue with me on this, and

I'd be perfectly content to think I was wrong. But that's why, facing my sense of honesty as a writer, and risking criticism, I felt I had to write it this way.

Partly because the original idea came so plainly from outside, I assumed while I was writing that this was one of the least personal of my novels. It was only months later, reading it with all the distance cold print brings, that I realised this was the year my youngest child went off to university. After twenty-two years, I'd reached the light at the end of the child-rearing tunnel at last. So a lot of my hero Simon Martin's experiences – his joys and frustrations – echo my own. And though there's a good thirty years in age between us, I'll unashamedly admit some of his sheer exhilaration at the end mirrors mine.

Anne Fine

THE CHARACTERS

The students

SIMON MARTIN – Famed only for sporting success and lack of application in all other fields.

WAYNE DRISCOLL – Simon's best friend and fellow football team member. Wayne is casual and easy-going.

MARTIN SIMON – A new boy. Weedy, intellectual and fond of poetry.

RUSS MOULD – Not very bright.

ROBIN FOSTER – Tense, excitable.

SAJID MAHMOUD – A born entrepreneur, inventive and energetic.

FROGGIE HAYNES – A bit of a tease.

GWYNN PHILLIPS – An embittered, self-pitying streak spoils his nature.

GEORGE SPALDER – Cheerful and amiable.

ROY FULLER – Sensible.

RICK TULLIS – Sullen and unforthcoming. And usually absent.

The teachers

MR CARTRIGHT – Nothing surprises him any longer. But he has his moods, and a phenomenally loud bellow.

MISS ARNOTT – Young and inexperienced, she is on the verge of breakdown, swigging aspirins constantly.

DR FELTHAM – Sets the highest academic standards, especially in sciences and maths.

MR KING – Teaches music.

MR HIGHAM.

Other characters

MRS MARTIN – Simon's mother.

SUE – Simon's mother's best friend and tennis partner.

HYACINTH SPICER – A much disliked neighbour of Simon's age.

MACPHERSON – Simon's dog, may be played by a stuffed toy.

FLOUR BABIES

ACT ONE

Most of the action of the play takes place in a boys' secondary school. In this particular academic year, the clever and industrious students are snapped up by Dr Feltham. The great majority are shared between Mr King and Mr Higham's classes. And the idle, inept and downright criminal fetch up with Mr Cartright. Simon's home is a clean, bright house on a city estate. The cramped back yard is shared with the Spicers next door.

SCENE ONE

*At the school, in the corridor. **Martin Simon** is wandering nervously down the corridor, carrying a stuffed schoolbag, and looking back indecisively over his shoulder. He collides with **Miss Arnott**, who is frantically shaking aspirins into her palm.*

MISS ARNOTT *shrieking in fright* Oh!

MARTIN Sorry, Miss.

MISS ARNOTT Oh! My nerves!

She throws the aspirins into her mouth.

MARTIN Miss? Please, Miss, I –

MISS ARNOTT Who are you? I've never seen you before. What are you doing here?

MARTIN I'm new.

MISS ARNOTT What's your name?

MARTIN Martin. Martin Simon.

MISS ARNOTT Well, at least it's not Simon Martin!

MARTIN Excuse me?

MISS ARNOTT Nothing. What are you doing down this corridor, anyway?

MARTIN I'm looking for my classroom.

MISS ARNOTT Well, it won't be down here. *She points.* All the science rooms are that way, though, Lord knows, you can hardly squeeze into them for all Dr Feltham's gubbins for the school Science Fair. And Mr King and Mr Higham's rooms are back that way, too. There's no point in your coming along here. Behind that door is Mr Cartright's class.

Martin Simon inspects the slip of paper in his hand.

MARTIN That's right. Mr Cartright's class.

MISS ARNOTT Really? Mr Cartright's? *She snatches the paper and studies it.* **Very** strange …

MARTIN *even more nervous now* Why?

MISS ARNOTT Well, you just don't look the type.

MARTIN The type?

MISS ARNOTT To be in Mr Cartright's class. I mean, look at you! What's all that making your bag bulge?

MARTIN Books.

MISS ARNOTT *astonished* **Books**? *She takes one out.* What's this, then? **Baudelaire**? It's in **French**. *She stares at Martin Simon accusingly* You read French!

MARTIN *guiltily* Yes.

MISS ARNOTT See? You won't fit in at all. Not in Mr Cartright's class. Still, it's your funeral.

She hurries off, shaking her aspirins.

MARTIN *really worried now* Funeral …?

He stands for a moment in silence, buries the book in his bag, takes a deep breath and pushes the door open. Instantly, we hear pandemonium.

SCENE TWO

In Mr Cartright's classroom. **Wayne Driscoll, Russ Mould, Robin Foster, Sajid Mahmoud, Froggie Haynes, Gwynn Phillips, George Spalder, Roy Fuller** *and* **Rick Tullis** *are paper-flicking, chair-rocking, desk-stabbing, yelling, leaning out of the windows, sleeping, card-playing, ball-tossing, arm-wrestling, arguing, etc.*

WAYNE Where's Simon? Anyone seen Simon?

FROGGIE What's the matter, Wayne? Lost your minder?

WAYNE Sajid? You seen Simon?

Martin Simon creeps in, unnoticed, and takes an empty desk at the back.

SAJID Saw him last night at football, didn't I?

WAYNE You great ear'ole! **I** saw him last night at football. I'm talking about **today**.

Martin Simon takes out his book, and puts his fingers in his ears.

ROY Got up late, maybe.

ROBIN Pretty late! Old Carthorse will be here in a minute.

The door smashes back on its hinges. **Mr Cartright** *comes in.*

MR CARTRIGHT *bellowing* Qui-ET! *There is instant and total silence* I said **QUIET!!!** *Then, realising* Oh! Sorry, lads. Wasn't expecting it to be so easy. Expect your mothers have been knocking you into shape over the holidays. Take off that scarf, Wayne Driscoll. Spit that gum out, Russ Mould. **Not** on the floor. In the bin. Where's Simon Martin?

WAYNE He's –

MR CARTRIGHT Get that chair's legs back on the floor, Sajid. All four of them. I'm watching you, Gwynn Phillips. Don't think I'm not. *He slams his files down on the desk* Right! Listen, everybody! And that means you, too,

3

Froggie Haynes. Do you want me to separate you two? The first thing we're doing – after waking up, George Spalder! – is to choose this class's option for the school Science Fair. I hope you're listening to this carefully, Sajid Mahmoud. I don't want to have to go over it again in your break time! It appears that Dr Feltham, in his **infinite** wisdom, has decided that this class is, after all, going to be allowed to take part.

GEORGE   What? Even after last year?

MR CARTRIGHT   Yes. Even after that disgraceful, not to say downright **dangerous**, exhibition last year.

WAYNE   That was **great**!

MR CARTRIGHT   As I remember, Wayne Driscoll, it was also very nearly the death of you.

WAYNE   But it was **great**.

RUSS   Ours was good, too. Remember our Soap Factory?

SAJID   Yes! Foster ate his lump for a dare.

ROBIN   *proudly*   Sick **eight times**!

GEORGE   We had a good laugh.

FROGGIE   You should have seen your face, Robin. It was pale as a maggot.

GEORGE   Maggots! Yes!

ROBIN   Yes! Maggot Farm! Maggot Farm!

MR CARTRIGHT   No, we're **not** doing the Maggot Farm.

ROBIN   Good thing, because my mum wouldn't even **look** at it. She said it was **disgusting**.

GWYNN   Should have put Sajid in charge of it. Would have had the maggots trained by the second day.

Sajid stands up to take a bow.

WAYNE   Sir! Sir! If we can't do the Maggot Farm, can we do the Exploding Custard Tins?

ROBIN   Yes! Yes! The exploding custard tins! They were great!

SAJID   Dead brilliant!

FROGGIE   Hooper's brother nearly burned his hand off.

GEORGE   Chop lost an eyebrow.

RUSS   Grew back different.

MR CARTRIGHT   No, I'm afraid the Exploding Custard Tins are out. No Soap Factory. No Maggot Farm. No Exploding Custard Tins.

WAYNE   Why not?

MR CARTRIGHT   After the shocking – not to say **explosive** – events of last year, Dr Feltham has decided that the laboratories will only be made available to those who passed their exams. Did anyone here pass Physics? Raise your hand.

Martin Simon tentatively raises his hand. Then, seeing he is the only one, he snatches it down again.

MR CARTRIGHT   Just as I thought. So. No more Exploding Custard Tins for you lot, I'm afraid. Anyone pass Chemistry?

*Again, **Martin Simon** is the only one to raise a hand, and, thinking better of it, he pulls it down again.*

MR CARTRIGHT   No surprises there. Goodbye Soap Factory. How was our record in Biology? Anyone have any luck there?

Martin Simon makes only a feeble gesture.

MR CARTRIGHT   Sadly, then, no Maggot Farm for us.

GWYNN   It's not fair, sir!

SAJID   No, it's not fair!

MR CARTRIGHT   Now, really, boys! You can't say you weren't warned. I fetch my coffee from the staff room. I have ears. I heard every one of your teachers saying it, over and over again: 'If they don't work, they'll end up in Mr Cartright's class.' And here you are.

GEORGE   You can't help it if you're stupid.

MR CARTRIGHT   If you lot were half as stupid as you act, you'd be on life-support systems.

GEORGE   That's not very nice.

MR CARTRIGHT   It's just a fact, George. After all, no one is here by accident.

MARTIN   I think **I** might be, sir.

Silence

MR CARTRIGHT   Who was that?

MARTIN Me, sir.

Martin lifts his hand.

MR CARTRIGHT You. Who are you?

MARTIN I'm new, sir.

MR CARTRIGHT Yes, I can see that. What's your name.

MARTIN Martin, sir. Martin Simon.

MR CARTRIGHT And what's that on your desk?

MARTIN A book, sir.

MR CARTRIGHT And what were you doing with it, Martin?

MARTIN *mystified* Reading it, sir. Reading it quietly.

MR CARTRIGHT Reading it quietly, eh? And without being asked, too. There's something very wrong here. Very wrong indeed. *He strides over and snatches up the book* Baudelaire! It's poetry! *Opening it* And it's in French! You're sitting here quietly, reading French poetry! In French!

MARTIN *Guiltily* Yes, sir. Sorry, sir.

MR CARTRIGHT Oh, so am I, lad. So am I! *Sighs* Well, what are you waiting for? Off you go.

MARTIN Where, sir?

MR CARTRIGHT You could try Mr King's class, I suppose. Or Mr Higham's. But I'm afraid you can't stay here.

MARTIN Why not, sir?

MR CARTRIGHT Well, it's obvious, isn't it? You don't fit in at all. You don't belong. For one thing, you enjoy reading. You'll be right out of place here for that alone. Then there's the other problem. You read French. Well, I admit there's quite a lot of language in this classroom. I, for one, have a temper. And there's the colourful patois of our local housing estate to be contended with.

SAJID And I can swear in three separate dialects, sir!

MR CARTRIGHT See? Plenty of language. But no French.

ROBIN He passed all those exams, too, sir. He put his hand up. I saw him.

MR CARTRIGHT Did he, indeed? Well, that settles it. He can't stay here. If he's going to go round passing exams, maybe he even ought to think of trying Dr Feltham's class.

*There are expressions of shock, sharp intakes of breath, etc. Regretfully, **Martin** packs and makes for the door*

MR CARTRIGHT   Believe me, lad, it's for the best. Tell the office they've got it all wrong. It's Simon Martin who ought to have his bum on that seat, not Martin Simon. Tell them it's a clerical error, and they're to find you a proper home.

MARTIN   Yes, sir. Goodbye, sir.

MR CARTRIGHT   *wistfully*   Goodbye, lad. Good luck! *He swings round to quell the rising chaos*   Right! Shut that noise! Stop tunnelling through your desk lid, Froggie Haynes. That's school property, that is. We're getting this Science Fair business sorted out before the bell rings, or no one will get their break time. As far as I can make out from his notes, Dr Feltham has given us five choices.

ROY   Five? That's not bad.

MR CARTRIGHT   Wait till you hear. We can do any one of the following: Textiles; Nutrition; Domestic Economy; Child Development; Consumer Studies.

WAYNE   Boring!

ROBIN   You can't call that lot 'Science'. It's not right.

RUSS   I don't even know what half of them **mean**.

MR CARTRIGHT   Translation for Russ: Sewing; Food; Shopping; Babies and so forth; Thrift.

RUSS   Frift? What's frift?

SAJID   Dr Feltham's just trying to pick on us. We can't do babies and sewing and shopping!

MR CARTRIGHT   Not all of them. One of them. We just have to choose.

WAYNE   We're not choosing any of those. They're all **stupid**.

ROBIN   *sarcastically*   Oh, excuse me! We're Table 14 in the Science Fair. Please come and look at our nice sewn-on buttons!

RICK   I'm not coming in to do rubbish stuff like that!

RUSS   You hardly ever come in anyway.

RICK That's not the point, Mould!

MR CARTRIGHT Somebody must have a preference. What about you, Robin?

ROBIN Oh, no, sir. I'm not choosing. I know what'll happen to the person who chooses. They'll be hated by everybody all term. They'll get mashed.

GWYNN Seriously maimed.

RICK I'll help anyone bash them.

WAYNE So will I.

GEORGE Me, too.

MR CARTRIGHT *cunningly* Right, then. I have a good plan. The very next boy responsible for any disturbance in this classroom – any noise or interruption at all – will have to choose one of these cards, and whatever is written on it is what we will do.

ROBIN What? Even **babies**?

MR CARTRIGHT Even babies.

SAJID That isn't fair, sir.

WAYNE Starting when?

MR CARTRIGHT Starting **now**.

Instant silence. With a look of disgust, Mr Cartright inspects the five cards. There is the most tremendous rattle and thump at the door. **Simon Martin** *strides in, whistling, and knocks over a whole pile of books on a desk, a pot of rulers, a box of cassettes, etc. Sensing the silence and the stares, he freezes.*

SIMON What've I done? Why are you all staring at me? What've I done?

MR CARTRIGHT Nothing, lad. It's just that you are the lucky person who gets to pick a card.

Everyone else relaxes.

SIMON What? Like a raffle prize?

MR CARTRIGHT Not quite.

WAYNE Where've you been, Sime?

GEORGE Last one in class gets maimed.

ROBIN Saved a place for you, Simon!

FROGGIE Found us at last, have you, you great fishcake!

8

RUSS   Get a brain, Sime!

MR CARTRIGHT   Why are you twenty minutes late?

SIMON   Got stuck, didn't I? In Dr Feltham's class.

ROBIN   *horrified*   Dr Feltham's!

SIMON   Told him I didn't belong. But would he listen? Not him. Not till that other ear'ole came along and rescued me.

MR CARTRIGHT   Do you mean Martin Simon?

SIMON   I dunno. But he was as sad as the others. Do you know what they were doing, sir? Revision of multiplication of improper fractions, sir. On the first day!

ROBIN   That's cruel, that is.

SAJID   Shocking!

MR CARTRIGHT   Never mind, boy. It's all over now. You're safe back here. So pick a card.

Simon picks a card and attempts to read it out.

SIMON   Chile . . . Chile . . . Devlopment.

MR CARTRIGHT   Child Deve**lop**ment.

SIMON   What I **said**, yes.

ROBIN   That's **babies**, that is!

WAYNE   You can't call it science! It's a great big cheat!

SAJID   Pick again, Sime!

RICK   I shan't be coming in at all now. Not till it's all over, anyhow.

MR CARTRIGHT   And the experiment Dr Feltham has chosen for this topic is: **Flour Babies**.

ROY   Is that **flour** babies or **flower** babies?

RUSS   What's Roy mean?

ROBIN   Get a brain, Russ.

MR CARTRIGHT   Just a second, lads! Give me a minute to look it up.   *He leafs through the notes, finds it, reads. A look of horror crosses his face*   My God! I don't believe it! I do not believe it! Oh, this is unimaginable! This is out of the question, this!

Their faces have lit up. They exchange glances.

FROGGIE   Sounds quite good really.

GWYNN   Might be better than the Maggot Farm.

MR CARTRIGHT   Well, we're not doing it! Oh, no, no, no! Over my dead body!

WAYNE   Sounds dead brilliant.

MR CARTRIGHT   You can forget it, Wayne.

WAYNE   But you did promise, sir! You said! Sime picked it fair and square! You can't change now!

SIMON   *chanting*   Flour Babies! Flour Babies! Flour Babies! Flour Babies!

EVERYONE   *chanting*   Flour Babies! Flour Babies! Flour Babies! Flour Babies!

MR CARTRIGHT   SILENCE!!!   *Steaming with rage*   Oh, Dr Feltham, I'm an equable man, but, really, this time you have gone too far!   *He strides to the door*   Now I want absolute silence while I'm out. Understand? Absolute silence!

Mr Cartright slams out. There is absolute silence for five seconds, then, in an instant, the same noise and riot with which the scene began.

SCENE THREE

*In the corridor. **Dr Feltham** is striding along, carrying a large piece of equipment. **Mr Cartright** catches his arm.*

MR CARTRIGHT   Whoa, Feltham! Just a cotton-picking minute. I want a word with you.

DR FELTHAM   Is there a problem, Eric? I'm in a bit of a hurry to get Wishart's Digital Sine-Wave Generator along to the –

MR CARTRIGHT   Damn Wishart's Digital Wave-Sine Thingummy! What I –

DR FELTHAM   Sine-Wave, Eric. Sine-Wave.

MR CARTRIGHT   Whatever! What about these **Flour Babies**?

DR FELTHAM   What about them, Eric? They're just a simple experiment in parent and child relationships. Each boy takes full responsibility for his flour baby for two

10

whole weeks, keeping a diary to chart his problems and attitudes. It's fascinating what they learn.

MR CARTRIGHT One thing you'll learn, Feltham, is that not one of the boys behind that door could take care of a **stone** without cracking it. I know you said you'd never have them in the laboratories again. But why can't they do something in the workshops?

DR FELTHAM Eric, the workshops are buzzing! Why, there's the slopes to put up for the slope friction experiment. And the skeleton house to build for Percival's electronic burglar alarm system. The base for Harrison's thermistor-powered fan hasn't even been begun yet. Nor has the frame for the Huggett twins' electric power station.

MR CARTRIGHT *pleading* Please, George. I'm begging you.

DR FELTHAM I'm sorry, Eric. It's more than my job's worth to let your crowd into the workshops at the moment. Last time I frisked Rick Tullis on the way out, he had four of my screwdrivers down his underpants. Four! And that Sajid Mahmoud of yours only has to **look** at a wood plane for its blade to slip out of true. I'm sorry, Eric. But, no. And the flour babies are really a very worthwhile experiment. You wait and see.

The classroom door opens. Simon's head sticks out.

MR CARTRIGHT Wait and see? *Tapping the Science Fair file* According to what you've got in here, the only thing I'm likely to see is fifty pounds of sifted white flour exploding in my classroom!

*A look of rapture crosses **Simon's** face.*

SIMON *softly* Fifty pounds of flour! Exploding! In the classroom! Oh, magic!

MR CARTRIGHT Shut that door, Simon Martin, before I come and shut it for you with your face still there!

*Hastily, **Simon** withdraws. **Dr Feltham** tries to get away, and **Mr Cartright** pursues him.*

MR CARTRIGHT I can't believe you're doing this to me, George. All those bags of flour. In my classroom. With that pack of psychopaths. You must be off your trolley!

DR FELTHAM   Eric, stop fretting! It'll be all right, I promise you. Now come along with me, and get them now.

MR CARTRIGHT   Get what?

DR FELTHAM   The flour babies. They're back in my room.

MR CARTRIGHT   I'm not helping you carry that – that – that heavy thing you're carrying.

DR FELTHAM   Wishart's Digital Sine-Wave Generator.

MR CARTRIGHT   Whatever.

*They go off together, **Mr Cartright** complaining till they are out of hearing.*

MR CARTRIGHT   I'm warning you, George. You can push a man too far. And I shan't forget this. If you are ever in a jam, don't come to me. I shan't forget this. No, I shan't forget.

SCENE FOUR

*In **Mr Cartright's** classroom. **Simon** pulls his head in from the doorway and speaks to the class.*

SIMON   Them flour babies! They're dead brilliant! They're an explosion. Like the custard tins.

ROBIN   *ecstatic*   Custard Tins II!

ROY   How do you know?

SIMON   Just heard. I was earwigging out the door, and I heard Carthorse say so.

RUSS   Exploding flour!

SAJID   Magic! Imagine!

SIMON   The floor would be knee-deep in it.

ROBIN   *throwing up his arms*   Flour rain!

GEORGE   Puff! Puff! Out of the door! Along the corridors!

WAYNE   Like an atomic explosion.

FROGGIE   Mushroom flour cloud.

ROBIN   Sounds **excellent**.

*Gwynn inspects the cards on **Mr Cartright's** desk.*

GWYNN   Yes, but some of these other things might be even better. If we do textiles, we could get to use the sewing machine, and make it go so fast, it busts.

RICK   I could make a Nazi flag.

GEORGE   Don't be such a stain, Rick.

SAJID   Stains! Stains! If we did textiles, then we could do stains. I can think of some stains that would never come out. Ever!

ROBIN   On the other hand, in consumer studies, you're let off down the shops.

FROGGIE   Do you remember when only four of us bothered to come back, and poor Miss Arnott took a major fit.

ROBIN   Finished her aspirins.

RUSS   Had to send us out again, to get some more.

GWYNN   *still inspecting the cards*   What's domestic economy?

FROGGIE   *scornfully*   Wendy Houses.

ROBIN   *in a high voice*   'Oh, no! Don't use that cloth to wipe the plates! You just used it down the lavatory!'

ROY   'Fetch in your washing when it rains, or it might get wet again!'

RUSS   *reading the card*   How about noot – noot –

ROY   Nutrition. Food to you, Russ.

SAJID   Nutrition doesn't have anything to do with food.

FROGGIE   'Course it does.

SAJID   No, it doesn't. It's all just looking at charts and stuff. We did it last year.

WAYNE   Balanced meals! What two old codgers with wobbly teeth would have for lunch.

ROBIN   And turning ounces into grams.

SAJID   And grams back into ounces.

ROBIN   On and on. Never got round to cooking anything.

SAJID   I got to cook once. Then got in a giant great row for scraping it in the bin straight after it was marked.

SIMON   What did you do that for?

SAJID   Well, I couldn't eat it, could I? It was meat stew, and I'm a veggie.

GWYNN Should have cooked something different.

SAJID Why? Nobody said a thing about **eating** it. Nobody even so much as **mentioned** eating it. They went on and on about it being all well-balanced, like Wayne says, and having vitamins and such. But nobody ever said a thing about liking it or eating it.

SIMON So let's just do the flour babies. They're the best.

GWYNN *suspiciously* Are you **sure** it's explosions, Sime? Because, if it isn't, you're in major trouble.

RICK I'll help you bash him. I'll come in for it, special.

SIMON There'll be no need for bashing. It'll be brilliant. Just you wait and see.

Leaping on a chair, he throws out his arms with visionary fervour. They all stare, mesmerized.

It'll be over a hundred pounds of glorious, snow-white sifted flour, spinning all over, floating, swirling. It'll be a snow-storm, a blizzard, and we'll be snowmen, yetis, walking avalanches. It'll be glorious. A glorious, glorious, explos –

Mr Cartright bursts in, dragging a large black bin bag.

MR CARTRIGHT **Off** that chair, Simon Martin. That's school property, to be treated with respect. Bums on your seats, lads, while we get all this flour baby business sorted. *He pauses, hopefully* Unless, by any chance, you've changed your minds . . .?

SIMON No, sir! It's flour babies. It's agreed.

EVERYONE *chanting* Flour babies! Flour babies! Flour babies!

Mr Cartright pulls them out of the bag, one by one, tossing them at speed round the room. Some are plain six-pound hessian sacks. Others have eyes drawn on. One has large eyes with long eyelashes, and a frilly frock and bonnet.

MR CARTRIGHT Catch, Driscoll! Mould! Foster! Here's yours, Phillips! Tullis! Nearly didn't bother to get one for you, you're so rarely here. Fuller! Martin! Simon Martin! Catch, dozy! Aren't you supposed to be one of the school's sporting heroes?

Left-handed, **Simon** *catches the spinning frilly flour bag.*
Robin *immediately starts comparing his with* **Simon's.**

MR CARTRIGHT   Mahmoud! Your flour baby. Catch!

ROBIN   Sir! Sir! How come Simon gets one with eyes?
Mine's just plain boring old sacking. And his is dressed.
It's got a frock and bonnet and everything. And mine's got
nothing. It's not fair.

MR CARTRIGHT   Listen, Robin. If every parent who had
a baby who was a bit lacking sent it back, this classroom
would be practically empty. Sit down and be quiet.   *He*
tosses out the last two bags   George Spalder. Froggie
Haynes. And that's the lot.

GEORGE   But what are we supposed to do with them,
sir?

MR CARTRIGHT   I'm coming to that, aren't I? Now,
everybody sit quietly while I read out the rules.

RICK   *horrified*   Rules?

GWYNN   *disgusted*   Rules!

MR CARTRIGHT   Of course, rules. This is an
experiment, boys.   *Reading*   **'Rule 1. The flour
babies must be kept clean and dry at all times.
All fraying, staining and leakage of stuffing will be
taken very seriously indeed.'**

RUSS   Mine's already dirty, sir. Wayne's just splattered it
all over from his cartridge.

MR CARTRIGHT   **'Rule 2. The flour babies will be
weighed regularly to check for weight loss that
indicates neglect or maltreatment, and weight gain
that suggests tampering or damp.'**

RUSS   What's tampering?

FROGGIE   Shame, Robin. You won't be able to keep your
pet marble collection in yours.

MR CARTRIGHT   QUI-ET! **'Rule 3. No flour baby may
be left unattended at any time, day or night.'**

SIMON   Day or night?

WAYNE   *horrified*   We're not taking them home, are we?

MR CARTRIGHT   **'And if you must be out of sight
of your flour baby, even for a short while, a
responsible babysitter must be arranged.'**

15

GEORGE   Oh, come on!

RICK   I don't believe this.

MR CARTRIGHT   'Rule 4. Everyone must keep a **Baby Book, and write in it daily. Each entry should be no shorter than three full sentences.'**

RUSS   That's going to be the worst bit.

WAYNE   If only!

MR CARTRIGHT   I'll give you your Baby Books now.

He roots in the bin bag.

RICK   Did anybody hear the word 'explosion' in all that?

GWYNN   I never heard it.

FROGGIE   Neither did I.

GWYNN   We're warning you, Simon. You had better be right about this explosion business. Or you are seriously sunk.

RICK   Seriously!

FROGGIE   Are you hearing this, Simon?

GWYNN   Simon!

Simon isn't listening. He's cocked his head on one side, and he's cooing to his flour baby, picking bits of fluff off her frock.

SIMON   There you are, sweetheart. That's better, isn't it? Nasty old bits of fluff and horrid old rubber droppings all over your pretty frock and your pretty bonnet.

ROBIN   *concerned*   Simon?

SIMON   And where's my poppet going to sit? Let's get this nasty, grubby old patch of desk cleared up for you.   *He turns to Robin. Everyone falls silent and stares. Sternly* Foster, she's already getting grubby. Now I'm warning you, you're going to have to keep this desk a whole lot cleaner in future, and I mean that.

Robin's mouth drops open. Then, recovering himself, he affects terror, draws away, and puts his hand up for attention.

ROBIN   Sir! Sir! You're going to have to move me! I can't stay here. It's not safe. Simon Martin's turning into my mother!

The room erupts into riot. Flour babies are tossed up and

16

down, amid jeering cries.

GWYNN AND OTHERS   Mrs Martin! Mrs Martin!

FROGGIE AND OTHERS   Good Old Mother Sime!

Mr Cartright slams both hands down on the desk.

MR CARTRIGHT   Quiet! You heard me! I said QUI-ET!!

*Clearly astonished at the reaction he's provoked, **Simon** clutches his flour baby protectively to his chest and stares.*

ACT TWO

SCENE ONE

In the Martins' kitchen, a week later. **Simon** *is sitting at the table, propping up his flour baby, prodding her till she falls over the edge, then catching her, over and over.*

SIMON   Ha! Can't even sit up yet! Whoopsie! Not very good at sticking up for yourself, are you?

Mrs Martin comes in with the laundry basket just as he misses the catch and the flour baby falls in the dog basket.

SIMON   Blast!

MRS MARTIN   You mustn't swear in front of it. You'll set it a bad example.

SIMON   Not it, Mum. Her.

Mrs Martin sorts laundry. There is even a pile for the flour baby.

MRS MARTIN   She gets through enough laundry in a week. You ought to keep her in a plastic bag.

SIMON   Is that what you did with me?

MRS MARTIN   I only wish I'd had the sense.

Simon picks the frilliest frock off the pile, and changes the flour baby.

SIMON   There we go, poppet. Big breath now. Pop your head out.

Mrs Martin rolls her eyes to heaven.

SIMON   What was I like, when I was her age, Mum?

MRS MARTIN   Oh, you were sweet. As good as gold, and chubby as a bun.

SIMON *bunching his biceps* No muscles, then?

MRS MARTIN No, no muscles. But you had bright little button eyes. You were so lovely that perfect strangers stopped me in the street to coo at you, and blow raspberries on your tummy.

SIMON Premier League, was I?

MRS MARTIN You were wonderful. You were the most beautiful baby in the world.

SIMON *suddenly sour* So why did my dad push off so quickly, then?

MRS MARTIN Be fair, Simon. He did hang around for six whole weeks.

SIMON It's not a joke, Mum. Tell me why he left.

MRS MARTIN Simon, you keep asking this, and I keep telling you. I don't know why he left.

SIMON How did he leave, then?

MRS MARTIN What do you mean, how?

SIMON Just that. How did he leave? If you don't know why, tell me how. What did he say? What did you say? Was Gran there? Was there a giant great row? Give me a clue, Mum. Tell me how.

MRS MARTIN *To the flour baby* This is your fault, you know. My lad was fine before you came along. And now look at him! Brooding away about his long lost father. I blame you.

SIMON It's not a joke, Mum. He is my father, and –

MRS MARTIN *sharply* Was, Simon.

SIMON *determinedly* Is, Mum. And so I have a right to know.

Mrs Martin softens. She pats his hand gently.

MRS MARTIN I know, Simon. And I am sorry. It's just that there's absolutely nothing to tell.

SIMON There must be. I didn't come out of nowhere. He was here. I know you didn't have a proper wedding, or anything. But there still ought to be some photographs.

MRS MARTIN Simon, there are photos. There are lots.

SIMON But not with him. There's hardly a single one of him.

19

MRS MARTIN   That's because he was usually the one holding the camera.

SIMON   You could have taken at least one good one of him.

MRS MARTIN   *angrily*   And how was I supposed to know that he was going to walk out on me? Women don't always get a week's notice, you know!

SIMON   Very convenient. He finishes with you. Never sends any money. Never writes. I bet, after all this time, even a private detective couldn't find him. And you finish with him. Definitely. But what about me? I haven't finished with him. There's still things I want to know. Things that I think about …

MRS MARTIN   *sadly*   Oh, Simon.

SIMON   So, tell me, Mum. Tell me about the day he left.

MRS MARTIN   There was nothing special about it, Simon. Nothing at all. He wasn't in a mood, or anything. We hadn't quarrelled. He got you up, cuddled you, dressed you –

SIMON   Didn't drop me on my head?

MRS MARTIN   He was always very good with you. Gentle. Careful. He could make you smile with his singing. He was singing while he got the breakfast that day, I remember.

SIMON   I didn't know he could cook.

MRS MARTIN   No, he couldn't. We had cornflakes. He was just chatting as usual. Normal stuff, all about next door's dog barking, and the post being late. That sort of thing. Then Sue came round. And halfway through the morning he strolled off, whistling, with his hands in his pockets. We thought he was going to get beer, or a bar of chocolate, or something.

SIMON   *thoughtfully*   And he never came back.

MRS MARTIN   He never came back. At first we thought something terrible must have happened. A road accident, maybe. But then I noticed the blue bag was missing. He must have packed it, lowered it out of the window on a rope, then sneaked round to the yard to fetch it while we were still waiting for hom to come in at the front.

SIMON   Maybe the bag just happened to get nicked that

day! Maybe he didn't just disappear. Maybe he was kidnapped! Or murdered! Or lost his memory! Or –

MRS MARTIN *gently* Simon, we found the rope. And all the little things he cared about had gone from the house.

Simon is clearly upset. Furiously, he dashes the tears off his cheeks and hides his head in his hands.

SIMON *almost too softly to hear* So what was he whistling?

MRS MARTIN Sorry?

SIMON *lifting his head* When he walked out. What was he whistling? What tune was it?

The phone rings in the hall.

MRS MARTIN Oh, Simon! How on earth should I remember something like that?

Mrs Martin goes out. Simon confides in the flour baby.

SIMON Why shouldn't she? It's no odder than remembering that he had cornflakes for breakfast that morning, is it? In fact, it's probably a clue. If you could work out what he was whistling, you might be able to work out why he left. Suppose he was singing 'Goin' to the City and Ain't Never Comin' Back'. You'd know he wasn't so much leaving you as moving on to something more exciting. *Pause* What? What did you say? *He lifts the flour baby until her mouth is close to his ear.* Yes, that is odd, isn't it? I've thought that, too. That if I hadn't been here, already born, just like you, then by now my dad would just be one of those dozens of old boyfriends that Mum's forgotten completely. She probably wouldn't even get his name right by now, if I hadn't been born. *He holds the flour baby to his ear again.* Yes, you're right. Babies make all the difference. Especially when they're as clever and beautiful as you!

Mrs Martin comes back and catches him nuzzling the flour baby.

MRS MARTIN Look at you! If one week with a dolly sends a great lad like you as soft as putty, what hope is there for any girl?

SIMON Who was that on the phone?

MRS MARTIN   Sue, coming to pick me up for tennis. Now, while I'm gone –

SIMON   *hastily*   I won't be here. I'm off to football practice.

MRS MARTIN   Make sure you put the little lady somewhere safe.

SIMON   Mum! I'm not taking her again! I told you what happened last week. It was dire! I couldn't concentrate. I was worrying about her all the time. Wondering if those thugs in Mr King's class were using her as a football in the changing rooms. Having visions of her dumped facedown in the sink. Imagining that animal Holdcroft drawing a moustache on her with his magic marker. I couldn't go through all that again, Mum. I really couldn't.

MRS MARTIN   That's just part of the job, Simon. You'll soon get used to it.

SIMON   How can you get used to having Horror Show visions each time you park someone out of sight for twenty seconds?

MRS MARTIN   You just do. Because it happens all the time.

SIMON   Really? Did you have this with me?

MRS MARTIN   Everyone has it, Simon. Why do you think you see so many grim-faced mothers dragging babies in pushchairs where pushchairs clearly aren't designed to go?

SIMON   I never thought.

MRS MARTIN   *grimly*   Nobody does. Until it happens to them.

SIMON   Well, it's not happening to me again. Last week I played the worst game I've ever played. No one can think about two things at once. You're always saying that, aren't you?   *Imitating*   'How can you be doing your homework properly if you're listening to that radio?' And they go on about it enough at school.   *Imitating*   'No one can talk and listen at the same time. If you're talking, you're not listening.' So why are you all suddenly so keen to let me get thrown off the team for not being able to think long enough to kick a ball straight?

MRS MARTIN   It's all part of the experiment, Simon.

SIMON   Well, it's a daft experiment, and I shall say so when I write in my Baby Book tonight. The fact is, you need two people to look after a baby. One person's not enough. You need a substitute. A good reserve. Someone with no particular plans for the evening.   *Firmly* Otherwise it simply can't be done.

MRS MARTIN   If it can't be done, how come you're still with us?

SIMON   *mystified*   What?

MRS MARTIN   There's only me. And you're still here, sound in wind and limb.

SIMON   *peering at himself*   So I am. How did you manage, then?

MRS MARTIN   Just did. I had to.

SIMON   Didn't you ever wish him back? To help?

MRS MARTIN   At the start, I did.

SIMON   What about that time I had mumps really badly?

MRS MARTIN   What about it?

SIMON   You wished him back then. I remember. *realising*   Mu-um! You just wanted him to catch them off me, out of spite!

MRS MARTIN   It's hard to miss someone who was hardly here. But I do think about him sometimes, when I hear a voice like his, singing. He had a voice to make the rafters ring.

Sue comes in, carrying her tennis racquet.

SUE   Who are you talking about? His dad?

SIMON   *astonished*   How did you guess?

SUE   Voice to make the rafters ring? Only one like that! Remember the song he was singing the day he left, Fran? *sings*   'Unfurl the sail, lads, and let the winds find me Breasting the soft, sunny, blue rising main –' Forgotten the rest.   *to Mrs Martin*   Got your racquet? Time to go.

SIMON   Mum! What's the next bit?

Mrs Martin searches the cupboard for her racquet.

MRS MARTIN   I'd completely forgotten. How did it go? *hums a snatch, then sings*   'Toss all my burdens and woes clear behind me, Vow I'll not carry those cargoes again.'

23

What's the next bit? No. Gone. See you, Simon. Don't forget to lock up.

Sue and *Mrs Martin* hurry out. *Simon* turns to his flour baby.

SIMON   They don't think, do they? It never occurs to them that this might be important to me. All Mum does is blame you for setting me off thinking, then rushes off to tennis. *He starts tugging the flour baby's bonnet straight, humming. The humming turns into the song.* 'Unfurl the sail, lads, and let the winds find me.' What was the next bit? Something about sunny mains. *hums* You see, I **do** miss him, in a funny sort of way, considering I never knew him. I mean, I have a picture of him in my mind, the way his eyes crinkle when he smiles, and the way he tosses a ball up and down in his left hand ... Do you know what I used to imagine? Every day, on my way home from school, I'd pretend he'd come back again. Just showed up, while I was out. And he and Mum would try again. And this time it would work, and he would stay. I'd think about it all the way home, and when I got near the corner, I'd slow up – start to drag my feet – so I could imagine it that little bit longer. And then I'd wipe him out, just like that, so I wouldn't be disappointed when I got home and found it wasn't true.

Simon lifts the flour baby's bonnet so he can look into her eyes.

Do you think I'm silly? Do you think I'm mad?   *Pause*   I just wish I knew why he left. Mum says it's nothing to do with me, but I'm not so sure. And maybe the song **is** a clue.   *Whistles, then bursts into song.*
'Unfurl the sail, lads, and let the winds find me ...'

HYACINTH   *off, singing*   'Breasting the soft, sunny, blue rising main –'

SIMON   Oh, just my luck if the only one to know it is Hyacinth Spicer. **Not** the most helpful person in the world ...

*He goes to the window, where **Hyacinth** appears.*

HYACINTH   Was that your Mum singing before? Not very good, is she?

SIMON   *cunningly*   It's a very hard song to sing.

24

HYACINTH   No, it isn't.

SIMON   Prove it, then. Sing the next bit.

HYACINTH   *singing*   'Toss all my burdens and woes clear behind me, Vow I'll not carry those cargoes again.' *dismissively*   And then it's just the chorus.

SIMON   Well, go on. Sing that.

HYACINTH   But anyone can sing that.

SIMON   I bet you can't. Not properly.

HYACINTH   Yes, I can. 'Sail for a sunrise that burns with new maybes, Farewell, my loved ones, and be of good cheer –' *breaking off*   What's this all about, anyway?

SIMON   *fiercely*   Sing, Hyacinth.

HYACINTH   *singing*   'Others may settle to dandle –' *breaking off again*   You really want to hear this, don't you? You want to know the words. Well, you're not getting the last line until I get that shoe you threw into the nettles.

SIMON   *exasperated*   Hyacinth, I've looked for that shoe of yours about a billion times.

HYACINTH   No shoe, no last line. You'd look a bit harder, I'd bet, if it were one of your football boots.

SIMON   Football!   *He slams the window shut*   Come on, sweetheart! We're late! Your second football practice coming up.   *He wraps her in his Tottenham Hotspur towel, making sure she can breathe easily, and see, and then goes round the room collecting his football gear.* Now, let me see, I explained all the rules to you last week, didn't I? Though I'm not sure you quite grasped the difference between an indirect free kick and a plain old corner. I'll explain that again, if you like. And it's a bit hoofy in the changing rooms, so I'll prop you up in that nice comfy bush at the goal end. Fresh air, you see. Good for you.   *Sternly*   And I hope you remember that this is a serious practice. Understand? No mucking about around the pitch. I certainly don't want to have to remind you how to behave.

As he leaves the house, locking the door behind him, we hear him whistling the tune.

SCENE TWO

At school in the corridor. **Sajid** *is pushing two huge battered prams lashed together with fuse wire. He runs into* **Miss Arnott**.

MISS ARNOTT   *shrieks*   Oooh!

SAJID   Sorry, Miss.

MISS ARNOTT   *rattling her aspirin bottle*   Sajid, what **is** this? No! Don't tell me! I don't want to know.

Clapping her hands over her ears, she hurries off. **Sajid** *stares at her departing back.*

SAJID   *gravely*   She's not going to last much longer. I can tell.

Simon *comes along and sees the pram contraption.*

SIMON   *admiringly*   Magic, Sajid! Have you tried it down the slope to the dining hall?

SAJID   I'm not trying to **break** it, Sime. I've only just gone to the trouble of making it.

SIMON   But why? What is it?

SAJID   That's obvious, isn't it? It's a pram.

SIMON   So why's it got eight wheels?

SAJID   Because it's actually two prams lashed together with some fuse wire Tullis nicked from Mr Higham's workshops.

SIMON   So if it's not for having a laugh on the slope, what's it for?

SAJID   Flour babies.

SIMON   *clutching his closer*   Flour babies?

SAJID   Don't be a dim bulb, Sime. It's a sort of travelling nursery for all the flour babies. You could fit all of them in here. They'd be a bit squashed, but you could stuff them in somehow. It's a crèche.

SIMON   More like a crush.

As they talk, **Sajid** *tries to round the corner. First the prams get stuck, then* **Sajid** *embarks on a laborious seven point turn.*

SAJID   The more the merrier. The more flour babies I stuff in, the more money I make.

SIMON   Money?

SAJID   *impatiently*   This crèche isn't going to run as a charity, Simon. If I'm taking responsibility, I'm taking money. That's business.

SIMON   Come off it, Sajid. No one will sign on for this. No one.

SAJID   Oh yes, they will. I've got most of the names down already, and the rest are going home tonight to sift through their moneyboxes and see if they can afford it.

Dr Feltham comes along, followed by several of his pupils carrying intricate and intimidating scientific equipment.

DR FELTHAM   And as for Hocking's Zero Gravity Project *He collides with the prams.*   Whoomph!

*He recovers, takes a breath to tell off **Sajid** and **Simon,** then gets distracted by the prams. He prowls around the strange contraption.*

DR FELTHAM   Now this is extraordinary. Quite extraordinary! And most fortuitous. Do you remember that only this morning, boys, we were discussing articulation in vehicles, and here is the perfect example of what I was trying to explain.   *To **Sajid***   Did you make this?

SAJID   *doubtfully*   Yes, sir.

DR FELTHAM   Well done! Well done!   *To his boys*   Note that, with a rigid rectangular structure of these propor-tions and eight wheels –   *Breaking off and pointing* What is this? Is this 30-amp fuse wire? I certainly hope it didn't come from any of Mr Higham's workshops! I shall check when I borrow it later to demonstrate the principles raised in this morning's lesson about angles of approach and separate speeds and velocities. But no time now. No time now!

*They hurry off. **Simon** and **Sajid** stare after them.*

SIMON   *pityingly*   Sad lives . . .

SAJID   Oh, yes, indeed. Sad lives . . .

They share a thoughtful pause. Simon recovers first.

SIMON *hopefully* Sure you don't want to try it on the slope before the bell rings? Be a good laugh.

SAJID *cracking* Oh, all right. But only once, mind. I don't want to ruin it.

Noisily, they go off together with the prams.

SCENE THREE

*In the classroom. The prams, ruined and muddy, are filled to overflowing with grubby flour babies. Only **Simon** still has his on his desk. **Mr Cartright** tosses a flour baby to **George**, who tosses it directly into the pram.*

MR CARTRIGHT There's yours, then, George. All tickety-boo. Now whose have I still missed? Ah, Gwynn! Toss it over, lad.

Gwynn picks his flour baby out of the crèche and tosses it to Mr Cartright, who throws it in the scales.

MR CARTRIGHT It's lost a bit. Nothing too critical, but you're going to have to watch it. A little bit of T.L.C. wouldn't come amiss.

Gwynn scowls horribly.

GEORGE What's T.L.C.?

MR CARTRIGHT Tender Loving Care.

FROGGIE Give it to Sime, then. He spends all day cuddling his dolly.

SIMON I do not!

MR CARTRIGHT Knock it off, lads. If that's the weighing over, it's time for our weekly browse through your Baby Books.

ROBIN Can I read mine first, sir? Can I? Can I?

MR CARTRIGHT Since he's deigned to honour us with his presence this morning, let's start with Rick Tullis. Rick, can we have your last entry, please?

RICK *reading sullenly* 'I said I wasn't coming in if we did this stupid baby thing, and if Mr Henderson hadn't spotted me down the shops, I wouldn't be here today. I definitely shan't be here tomorrow. Or the next day.

He sits down.

MR CARTRIGHT Is that it?

RICK Three sentences. That's what you said.

MR CARTRIGHT It's dispiriting, Rick. Truly dispiriting. A waste of time for you, and an unfair return for my efforts. No one in his right mind could consider the drivel you've written to be an adequate reward for my sheer teacherly grit, my unflagging fixity of purpose. Determinedly I stand here, day after day, term after term, trying to make you lads give of your very best. And what do I get? *Imitates* 'I shan't be here tomorrow. Or the next day. Or the next.' *He turns to* **Sajid.** Cheer me up, Sajid. Read me yours.

SAJID *proudly* 'I took my flour baby on the bus today. It was shoved under my arm, out of the way, till some interfering old trout —' *Slowly,* **Mr Cartright** *sinks into his seat and puts his head in his hands* '— forced me to sit down and put it on my lap. All the way she kept poking it and nattering to it. I thought she was a loony. But when we reached the Eye Centre, she got off. I certainly hope my eyes never go that bad.'

ROY You don't seem to have cheered him up much, Sajid.

SAJID He wasn't very happy about the crèche, either.

A sharp knock on the door. **Mr Cartright** *raises his head as* **Dr Feltham** *comes in.*

MR CARTRIGHT Ah, Dr Feltham. Welcome! Welcome! Excellent timing! Do step inside and hear one or two of our Baby Book entries.

DR FELTHAM I'm a bit rushed.

MR CARTRIGHT The boys will be so thrilled that you're taking an interest in this wonderful experiment of yours. Who shall we choose? Oh, yes! Let's have Simon Martin!

DR FELTHAM Simon Martin? Isn't he one of mine?

MR CARTRIGHT No, he isn't. The one **you** have is

called Martin Simon. You must know the boy. Passes exams, reads Baudelaire, that sort of thing. This one here is Simon Martin. Spends half his time skulking along the corridors on the way to the lavatories, and the other half acting a stick short of the full bundle.

DR FELTHAM *aside, reprovingly* I think you mean, Eric, that he's not yet living up to his full academic potential.

MR CARTRIGHT *not aside, cheerfully* Just what I said. Goes round behaving like a halfwit. Well, get on with it, Simon. Read Dr Feltham one of your diary entries. It's his experiment. He ought to know the sorts of things you lads are writing.

SIMON *reading* 'I thought my mum was a real meanie for not looking after my flour baby for a measly two hours while I did football. It's not as if she's as bad as a real one. Doesn't yell, or eat anything, or mess any nappies. And my mum's had enough practice looking after people. She's looked after me for 122,650 hours, if Foster's calculator works all right. And. unlike the flour baby, I yelled, and ate a lot, and made huge messes. Maybe that's why my dad only managed to stick a pathetic 1008 hours. Foster says that makes him 121.6765 times more of a meanie than my mum, but I reckon Foster may have pressed some of the wrong buttons.'

MR CARTRIGHT See? **See**? Is this really the sort of thing you had in mind?

DR FELTHAM But this is splendid, Eric! Absolutely splendid! Look what he's learned already. He's grasped that, even freed from three of the principal disadvantages of parenthood, the responsibilities are immense. He's learned a little about his own early childhood development. And he's even branched out into some quite sophisticated arithmetical calculations, working in tandem with this Foster.

*Simon braces his biceps proudly. **Mr Cartright** gnashes his teeth.*

MR CARTRIGHT *grimly* Read on, Simon. Read your next entry.

SIMON *reading* 'Today Macpherson my dog grabbed my

flour baby and gave her a bit of a chew at the bottom of our garden. Mum says I'm lucky he has such clean slobber and most of it came off. If I ever have a real baby, I will make sure it gets all its shots against rabies. And I am watching Macpherson very carefully indeed.'

DR FELTHAM   See, Eric? Learning about the staining capacity of canine salivary exudate on woven organic material.

MR CARTRIGHT   *scornfully*   Slobber on sacking!

DR FELTHAM   Exactly so! Not only that, but Simon here has already begun to reflect on the vital importance of primary childhood inoculation.   *Simon looks baffled but proud*   Indeed, he may even have gone to the trouble of looking up the first presenting symptoms of rabies. How else would he know what to look for in his dog?
To **Simon**   Did you go off to the library and look it all up, boy?

Simon looks astonished, then shrugs modestly and noncommittally.

MR CARTRIGHT   *icily*   Next entry, Simon?

Simon looks less confident.

SIMON   *reads*   'Today Froggie got hold of my flour baby for a bit of a muck-about so I called him an animal and stamped on his sandwiches. Then Mr Cartright puffed in, saving my flour baby from doom, and giving us both a detention'   *Pause. Then, to* **Dr Feltham**   Not me and the flour baby. Me and Froggie.

DR FELTHAM   *in disappointed tones*   A lot less learned yesterday, admittedly, Eric. We shall have to content ourselves with hoping the boy makes the very best use of his detention.

Simon scowls. Dr Feltham hurries out. And Mr Cartright shakes his head in astonishment.

MR CARTRIGHT   Well, **he** thinks you're learning something, obviously.

RICK   I've learned something. I've learned that people with babies have to be totally unhinged.

FROGGIE   Barking mad. I mean, they stroll round all day with these real ones tucked under their arms that keep bawling and messing and having to have their bums wiped –

RUSS   Not just their bums! My mum says you have to keep wiping their noses.

ROBIN   Grotesque!

GWYNN   Disgusting!

ROBIN   Just the thought of it makes you feel sick.

SAJID   And some of them are even heavier than ours. My aunt's weighs 24 pounds, and she still has to carry it. It still can't walk.

WAYNE   That's what gets me about them. They can't walk. They can't talk. They can't even get a spoon anywhere near their own faces, let alone kick a ball. I'm not surprised people used to dump them on mountains.

GEORGE   Or cook and eat them.

MR CARTRIGHT   No, I don't think so, George. Not cook and eat them.

GEORGE   Oh, yes, sir. They taste exactly like pork. I read it in a book.

GWYNN   What book? Do you still have it? Can I borrow it?

RUSS   What about crackling? Do babies make proper crackling?

FROGGIE   That might be a good reason for having one. I love crackling.

MR CARTRIGHT   Some people have babies by accident, don't forget.

ROY   Accident! How horrible! One slip, and your whole life ruined!

SAJID   And it might not even be your fault.

ROY   Best say no, if you're not sure.

GEORGE   Yes! Best say no! Not worth taking any risks!

WAYNE   One sloppy moment, and your life's not your own.

MR CARTRIGHT   *thoughtfully* I take it all back. Every word. You lot are learning something.

RICK   *sourly* What?

MR CARTRIGHT   Well, for one thing, you all seem to have learned that, though you're possibly old enough to father babies, you're certainly not old enough to be fathers.

FROGGIE   There's one of us hasn't learned that yet . . .

*They all stare at **Simon**, who is cuddling his flour baby.*

MR CARTRIGHT   *hastily*   Let's have another diary. How about you, George?

GEORGE   *reads*   'Bad times! I thought my flour bag was the pits, but next door have a real one. I hear it yowling through the wall. As I told Trish my goldfish, if it were mine, I'd tie its neck in a reef knot.'   *He waits for the roars of approval to subside. Reads*   'What gets me is that I get seriously ticked off for having my radio on so softly I can't even hear it. This baby is switched up to Volume 10 all night, and no one else complains. I went round to tell its mother that I wasn't getting much sleep, and she went totally unpicked. I only just managed to get off the doorstep ahead of the lava. I don't understand people with babies, really I don't. If that yowlbag was mine, I'd soon put an end to its bleating.

FROGGIE   Absolutely!

GWYNN   So would I.

ROBIN   So would anyone!

SIMON   I wouldn't.

ROBIN   Course you would! My Mum says she wouldn't like to count the number of times I nearly copped it from her, when I was teething.

GEORGE   Gran says her sister lost her temper once, and threw her baby in the cot so hard that one of its legs broke.

SAJID   The baby's? Or the cot's?

GEORGE   *suddenly confused*   Not sure.

SIMON   Well, my mum's friend Sue says she gets so ratty if she doesn't get a full eight hours uninterrupted sleep that it's a good thing she never had a family because, if she did, she'd murder all of them within a week.   *He picks up the flour baby and looks at her.*   And Mum went camping with Sue once, just for two nights, and came back saying she believed it.

ROBIN   There you are, then. Anyone can lose their rag with a baby.

SIMON   No. That's where you're all wrong. I couldn't. I know I couldn't.

FROGGIE   *jeering*   How do you know?

SIMON   *firmly*   I just **do**.

MR CARTRIGHT   You might think you feel that way, Simon. But –

Simon has risen to his feet, clutching his flour baby to his heart.

SIMON   No! You don't understand. I couldn't do it! Frankly, I don't even understand how anyone can get cross with a baby, let alone smack it, or yell at it, or – worse! – walk out on it one bright morning and never, ever come back! I don't know how anyone can do that, I really don't. *He lifts the flour baby up in front of his face with both hands. To the flour baby*   You do believe me, don't you? You know I'd never do that to you. Never, never, never! It's impossible! And I don't understand how **anyone** can do it.

He sinks to his seat, exhausted. They are all staring at him, concerned and silent. Before anyone can think of anything to say, the bell rings.

ACT THREE

SCENE ONE

At school in the corridor. A week later. **Wayne** *is squatting against the wall, scooping handfuls of soil from a plant pot and trying to trickle it through a hole in his flour baby's sacking. The plant in the pot leans pitifully to one side. We hear* **Simon** *singing lustily and getting closer.*

SIMON *offstage, singing* 'Sail for a sunrise that burns with new maybes. Farewell, my loved ones, and be of good cheer.'

He appears. His flour baby is carelessly stuffed upside down in his schoolbag.

'Others may settle to dandle their babies –'

He breaks off, sighs heavily, and starts the song again.

'Unfurl the sail, lads, and let the winds find me –'

The staff-room door opens. A wild-eyed, wild-haired **Miss Arnott** *stands there, rattling her aspirins.*

MISS ARNOTT Shut up! Shut up! This is the fourth time this morning you've wandered down this corridor singing, and missed out the last line. You're like that old Chinese water drip torture! If you must yodel all day, for God's sake finish the song before starting the damn thing all over again!

She slams the door shut.

SIMON *softly* OK, lady. Keep your hair on.

WAYNE *looking up* Why **do** you miss out the last line, anyway?

SIMON   I don't know it.

WAYNE   *nodding at the staff-room door*   You could ask her.

SIMON   And get my head bitten off? No, thanks. I think I'll wait till she calms down.

WAYNE   Don't leave it too long. She's obviously not going to last out very much longer.

SIMON   She's done quite well, considering.

WAYNE   Off sick a lot.

SIMON   Headaches.

WAYNE   Aspirin poisoning.

SIMON   Is that what you're trying to do to your flour baby? Poison it?

WAYNE   Don't be daft, Sime. I'm trying to get its weight up. It's just that the hole's too small to get much dirt in.

SIMON   Rip it bigger.

WAYNE   Oh, ace idea, Sime! Give Old Carthorse **two** reasons to maul me.

Simon pulls out his own flour baby.

SIMON   If you're in trouble, so am I. Mine looks in a lot worse shape than yours.

WAYNE   Strick, Sime! What a grime-bag! You'll catch it at the Great Weigh-in. *He takes **Simon's** flour baby and inspects it critically.*   You should never have let Hooper and Phillips use her as a goal marker.

SIMON   That didn't make much difference. What got her so torn was using her to tease Hyacinth Spicer's cat.

WAYNE   *dispassionately*   I don't think that the rips look nearly as bad as the chewed bits.

SIMON   I blame Macpherson. That dog's had it in for her right from the start. Jealous.

WAYNE   What about those black smudges?

SIMON   Fell in the grate, didn't she?

WAYNE   And the nasty charred bits?

SIMON   Oh, those are my fault. I left her on the grill while I made toast.

WAYNE   What about all this stuff stuck to her bum?

Simon takes her back and inspects her.

SIMON Glue. Lump of toffee. Mud. Macpherson's dried dribble. Chicken korma soup.

WAYNE *interrupting* It wasn't a fair experiment, really. We're not the type to do well, looking after babies.

SIMON I thought I was at first. But it turned out I was wrong. I guess some people are just good at looking after things, and others aren't. I must be out of the second box. *Sadly* A bit like my dad, perhaps. Start off firing on all cylinders, but can't keep up the pace.

WAYNE Shouldn't be blamed for it. Nobody's fault.

SIMON Just not the sort to settle and dandle our babies.

WAYNE *mystified* Come again, Sime?

SIMON *hastily* Nothing.

WAYNE *looking at his watch* Time to go.

SIMON I'll just brush off some of this slobber.

He spits on his thumb, and rubs a couple of stains further into his flour baby.

WAYNE You'll never get rid of those toothmarks.

Wayne goes off.

SIMON *to the flour baby* Macpherson only bit you because I spilt cornflakes on you. He was sucking you, really, except his stupid teeth got in the way.

*Enter **Mr King** and **Mr Higham**, carrying between them a large piece of technical equipment.*

SIMON So you mustn't get upset. You're still beautiful to me. Promise.

MR KING *aside* I tell you, that boy is seriously cracked.

MR HIGHAM *aside* I think he needs professional help.

MR KING *aside* Miss Arnott, would you believe it, thinks all this talking to his dolly business is 'rather sweet'.

MR HIGHAM *aside* That woman needs professional help as well. I wouldn't want to be around the day she runs out of aspirins!

They exit the other side.

SIMON Come on, then. Let's go and face the music. He can't expect you to look like Snow White after two whole weeks. Two weeks! That's getting on for half the time my dad looked after me. If you were me, you'd only have four more weeks of me, then I'd be off. It's hard to believe, really. I mean, look at you. By any standards, you're disgusting. And yet I'm still here, aren't I? Taking good care of you. What sort of little blot must **I** have been, that he didn't think I was worth staying around for?

Russ and Roy enter.

ROY Sime! Time to go! If you're late, you'll miss your weigh-in.

RUSS And the Grand Explosion!

Simon clutches his flour baby to his chest.

SIMON I might just skip that bit.

ROY *incredulously* Miss the explosion? Why?

RUSS Better than custard tins, you said.

SIMON It just doesn't sound such a good idea any more. I mean, I saw one this morning.

RUSS Custard tin?

ROY Explosion?

SIMON Baby!

RUSS What? A real one? Was it one of those purplish-blue ones you see on documentaries or one of those hulking great pink ones you see outside shops?

SIMON It was a pink one.

ROY I like the pink ones better.

RUSS More to explode!

SIMON Shut up, Russ!

ROY So what about this baby, Sime?

SIMON Well, I just made it laugh, that's all.

ROY How?

Simon raises one finger and waggles it.

SIMON Did that, didn't I?

Roy raises the same finger and waggles it.

ROY That?

SIMON   Yes.

Russ copies them.

RUSS   *incredulously*   Just that? And it laughed?

SIMON   Yup. One minute it had a little pudding face. I waggle one finger and suddenly it's like some mighty light bulb has switched on in its head. This baby's beaming at me as if I've turned a treble somersault with sparklers sticking out of my ears.

ROY   Well, that's babies for you.

SIMON   That's exactly my point. It seems a pity to explode them now.   *Cunningly*   After all, you'd never get something that good down the shops. Never.

ROY   Simon? Sime?   *He waves a hand in front of* **Simon's** *face.*   Anyone home in there? How can I put this, Simon? These flour babies are **not real**.

SIMON   *testily*   I know. I know.

ROY   But Mr Cartright is.

The bell rings.

SIMON   Oh, strick!

RUSS   Bad times! He told me next time I was late, he'd have my ears off.

All three run off.

SCENE TWO

In the classroom. **Mr Cartright** *has not arrived yet. There is the usual mayhem.*

GWYNN   Can I borrow someone's workbook?

ROY   Why?

GWYNN   To copy out yesterday's homework.

RICK   You don't want mine, then. I got the whole lot wrong.

WAYNE   You don't want mine, either. Old Carthorse told

me a brain-dead troll could have made a better stab at it.

GWYNN   All Carthorse said was that I had to **do** it. He didn't say anything about getting it **right**.

SAJID   You can borrow mine if you like. He never said it was rubbish so I think he must have liked it.

GWYNN   Right, then. I'll take yours.

He starts to copy it out. ***Froggie*** *rushes in.*

FROGGIE   Newsflash! Newsflash! Foster's just kicked his flour baby in the canal!

ROY   You're joking! Why?

FROGGIE   He couldn't help it. He just came unpicked.

ROY   Still! Kicking it in the canal!

SIMON   What happened?

FROGGIE   It sank, didn't it? One minute it was there in his bag. Next minute, an excellent penalty kick – *He traces the path of the ball through the air* – and it's in the water. Ten seconds later there is nothing to see but a few poky bubbles in the water.

SIMON   But why? What made him do it?

FROGGIE   It was the flour baby's fault. He spent all last night cleaning it up for this morning, and then the stupid thing goes and falls out of his bag onto the path, and gets all muddy again.

GWYNN   Well, fair enough!

SIMON   That's not the flour baby's fault! It's Robin's, for not looking after her properly!

ROY   Not her, Sime. It. I keep on having to tell you. They're not real.

Robin Foster *comes in. He is clearly in a foul temper.*

SIMON   Still, I don't see –

ROBIN   Don't see what, Sime? Don't see how anyone can get fed up with a stupid little flour bag and people going on and on at them all day? *Imitating* 'Don't forget it!' 'Take it here!' 'Take it there!' 'Make sure you strap it safely on your bike!' 'Don't lose it!' 'Keep it out of the mud!' 'Don't let it get wet!' 'Don't dirty it!' 'Make sure it doesn't fall!' 'Don't forget to pretend it's a real baby!' *He slams his fist down on the nearest desk* Well, all I did was pretend that it **was** real. And, if it was real, I'd have kicked it in the canal.

ROY Still, Robin. On the last day . . .

ROBIN I just lost my temper, didn't I? I just got sick of the stupid thing staring at me day after day.

SIMON Yours didn't stare. Yours didn't have any eyes.

ROBIN Oh, go walk the plank, Sime! It's all right for you. You don't mind going round acting like a major wally, chucking a six-pound bag of flour under the chin, and singing it lullabies.

SIMON Now, look here, Foster –

WAYNE No, Sime. **You** listen. Robin's right. I'm sick of mine as well. I'm sick of carrying it about everywhere I go, and trying to keep it dry and clean. I'm sick of the way it gets dirtier and dirtier without me even looking at it. I'm sick of putting it down somewhere perfectly all right for half an hour, and then, when I pick it up again, it's practically gone black. I tell you, I'd be as happy as Foster to boot mine in the canal!

SIMON No need for violence. What about Sajid's crèche?

WAYNE I haven't any more money!

GWYNN *bitterly* None of us have.

RUSS He's chiselled me out of weeks of my allowance.

FROGGIE Robbing us blind.

RICK Good as thieving, those prices.

SIMON Just owe him.

ROBIN Do us a favour, Sime. If you weren't so busy cuddling your dolly, you'd know he's hired two hard nuggets from the sixth form to poke the pram rent out of anyone who falls behind. *To Sajid* How much have you made so far, anyway?

SAJID *entirely unabashed* I should have made twice as much by now. But what with one or two people refusing to put their babies in, and Tullis forever being off, and me not thinking to start for the first week, and some people not coughing up what they owe in spite of me setting Henry and Luis on them, I only have –

He starts laboriously counting notes. They turn away in disgust.

ROBIN See? No wonder we're all broke.

GEORGE Yes. And I'm sick of walking home to save the bus fare, just so I can have a few measly hours off looking after that stupid flour bag. And I'm sick of getting no sympathy. Last night I was explaining how unfair it all was to my mother, and she just laughed. Laughed! Said she wished Sajid had been running his crèche when I was a baby. She'd have paid double his prices to get rid of me.

GWYNN You think that's a problem. I've had to wrap mine in a plastic bag twice a day to take it on the bike, just in case some idiot drove their car through a puddle and splashed it. I couldn't even think of going through a good puddle myself.

RUSS It's the naggers I can't stand. *Imitating* 'Don't forget to take it upstairs with you.' 'Don't forget to bring it down.' 'Don't leave it alone in the same room as the cat.' I **hate** the naggers.

SAJID Isn't that strange? I don't mind the naggers at all. It's the snoopers I hate. They go round pretending they're being friendly, but really they're telling you to do things differently. 'I'll tell you how I coped with mine', they say, all creepy smiles. Or, 'What I found worked best was this'.

ROBIN And you're supposed to smile back and pretend you're so thick you haven't realised that they're telling you off. Yes, I hate the snoopers too.

WAYNE I'll tell you what I can't understand. You can hardly open the paper without reading about someone who's been arrested for bashing a baby. And it's **never** the first time they did it. Well, I only had to give my flour baby a look, and my whole family were practically queuing up to phone the cops and snitch on me. So where do all these baby bashers live? Don't they have any family? Don't they have any friends?

RICK I hate my flour baby. I hate it more than anything else on earth. I can't wait to explode it. That's the only reason I'm in.

FROGGIE You're crazy if you believe Simon about this explosion business. He's got to be wrong. Old Carthorse has taught in this classroom for four hundred years. He isn't going to let anyone explode 50 pounds of white flour in here. He'd have to be out of his mind. It isn't going to happen.

RUSS *horrified* You really think Simon's got it all wrong?

SIMON But I heard him! I was earwigging from that door! 'Over fifty pounds of sifted white flour exploding in my classroom!' That's what he said. His exact words!

ROY I admit it doesn't sound Carthorse's sort of thing. But why else would they force us to look after these floppy useless flour bags for two whole weeks, if not to get us so boiling mad, we want to explode them?

GEORGE We were **told** why. It's to learn about ourselves, and how we feel about the job of being a parent. That was the whole point.

ROBIN Then it didn't matter me booting mine in the canal. Because I didn't learn anything. Not one single thing.

Mr Cartright walks in, unnoticed, and listens.

ROBIN All I learned is that I never, ever want a baby in my whole life unless someone else offers to look after it at least half the time, and there's a free crèche next door!

MR CARTRIGHT Now that's very interesting, Robin. Because I'm sure you'll know that, among women, that has become a common negotiating position and rallying cry. Anyway, I'm sure you'll all be relieved to know that I'm taking them back now.

GEORGE Taking them **back**?

ROBIN But what about the Glorious Explosion?

MR CARTRIGHT What glorious explosion?

ROY The one Simon promised us. He said you'd agreed it with Dr Feltham.

RUSS Better than custard tins, he said.

ROBIN Fifty pounds of sifted white flour exploding in his classroom. Whoof!

MR CARTRIGHT And you believed him? *He looks around at their faces.* You did, didn't you? You all believed him! *He turns to* **Simon**. You seriously managed to convince them that, on the last day, they'd get to see off fifty pounds of sifted white flour?

Simon nods.

MR CARTRIGHT *incredulously* In a Glorious
Explosion? Here, in my classroom?

Simon nods again. *Mr Cartright* begins to chuckle. The
chuckle grows into a series of great guffaws. He rocks with
laughter, clutching the sides of his desk, falls backwards off
his chair, sending the pot of steel rulers on his desk flying.
One hits the light fitting above. There is a glorious and pro-
longed explosion of sparks, blue flashes, hissing and spitting
wires. Suddenly nothing can be seen for smoke. Out of the
dead silence that follows comes a voice.

WAYNE *loyally* See? Simon was right.

SCENE THREE

At school, in the corridor. **Simon** *strides across the stage and
off again at the other side.*

SIMON *singing lustily* 'Others may settle to dandle
their babies –' *Pause* 'Unfurl the sail, lads, and let the
winds find me . . .'

The staff-room door flies open. **Miss Arnott** *rushes out.* **Mr
King** *follows her.*

MISS ARNOTT That's the fifth time he's traipsed past
this door, singing at the top of his voice. Why can't you
teach them quieter songs?

MR KING I never taught him that one. And what you
teach them makes no difference. The boys in his class
would belt out a cradle song as if it were a battle hymn.

MISS ARNOTT They call it a staff rest period. But really
it's just a different way of suffering. He sings right to the
end of the second-to-last line, and then stops dead. And
starts again at the beginning. *She rattles her aspirins*
I'm quite literally losing my mind.

MR KING Chopin had that problem once. Someone down-
stairs played a whole piano concerto late at night, and
then, when there was a knock on the door, broke off just

before the last chord. Poor Chopin tossed and turned, and then, at four in the morning, he cracked and rushed down to play the last chord very loudly. Then he went back to bed, and slept like a baby.

MISS ARNOTT   Really? Just after playing the one chord?

They go back in the staff-room and shut the door. **Simon** *returns. His singing is muffled by a bag worn over his head.* **Wayne** *runs on and whips off the bin bag.*

WAYNE   Sime! Red alert! I asked to go to the lavs so I could warn you. Rick and Gwynn and his thugs are out to get you because of this explosions business. They mean serious stuff. And Old Carthorse won't help you. He's ready to have your ears off. He's going to mash your brain.

SIMON   He was all right when he sent me to get the bin bag.

WAYNE   But then he started weighing in the flour babies. Now he's in free fall. Getting wilder and wilder. Gwynn's was practically empty. Russ had drawn a beard and moustache on his. And when he heard about Foster's being booted in the canal, he went positively incandescent and started flinging detentions about like confetti. When he sees your grubby little madam, he'll go unhinged.

SIMON   He can't expect her to look perfect. It's been two weeks!

WAYNE   I don't envy you going back in there, Sime. I wouldn't want to be in your shoes. Last time he was this bad, the walls shook so much, Miss Arnott's wall display came down.

They go off. Silence. The staff-room door opens. **Miss Arnott** *pops out her head and stares around warily, retreats, and shuts the door. Silence. The door opens.* **Miss Arnott** *does exactly the same again. The door closes. Silence.* **Simon** *and* **Wayne** *enter on tiptoe, dragging a massive and full bin bag.*

SIMON   Careful past this door. *Bitterly*   There's another wild animal in there.

WAYNE   I thought you got off rather lightly, considering.

SIMON   Oh, yes? Lightly? A week's detention?

WAYNE   I did warn you.

SIMON And I'm warning you. This one's in a real bate as well.

WAYNE It's not our fault she's not up to it. She should go off and have a baby if she's not a hard enough nugget to stick a punishing job.

SIMON *scornfully* Punishing job? It's quarter past eight till quarter past four. That's only – *fancy work on his fingers* – seven hours.

WAYNE *with even fancier finger work* Eight.

SIMON Still. Eight measly hours. If she can't hack that, she'd better not have a baby. Now there's a **real** job. Twenty-four hour shifts.

WAYNE Seven-day week.

SIMON No breaks.

WAYNE No holidays.

SIMON My mum says it's a life sentence. She says if, instead of having me, she'd stabbed someone to death with the breadknife, she'd have been well out of gaol by now. Twice over, if she'd been good.

WAYNE Dangerous business, having babies.

SIMON Slows you up.

WAYNE Ties you down.

SIMON Cramps your style.

WAYNE You'd think they'd be sick of us, wouldn't you? But most of the time, my mum and dad don't seem to mind. Except when I do something totally stupid.

SIMON Like when you fed your gran's wig to that alsation.

WAYNE What about when you threw that cactus at Hyacinth Spicer?

SIMON Yes, my mum was pretty wild about that. But most of the time she's quite fond of me really.

WAYNE I reckon that's how the trap works. First you know nothing. Then it's far too late. It's like you and your flour baby. That's why you've stuck it up your jumper and won't dump it in the bin bag with the rest.

SIMON *embarrassed* I didn't think anyone had noticed.

*Simon shifts his flour bag under his woolly as **Dr Feltham** strides in, carrying a large piece of equipment.*

46

DR FELTHAM *To Wayne* You, boy! Let me borrow you for a minute to help me get this to the labs.

WAYNE I'm already helping carry something, sir.

DR FELTHAM Listen, young man! These are Bernstein's Pressurized Cylinders! It's most important that they don't get tipped. Now let go of that rubbish bag you're dragging, and give me a hand here.

SIMON I'll wait for you. Okay?

Wayne goes off with Dr Feltham. Simon makes a comfy nest out of the bin bag, and settles in it. He hums, then, forgetting where he is, sings louder and louder.

'Sail for a sunrise that burns with new maybes. Farewell, my loved ones, and be of good cheer. Others may settle to dandle their babies –'

The staff-room door flies open. Miss Arnott sticks her head out.

MISS ARNOTT *singing hysterically* 'My heart's a tall ship, and high winds are near!'

Simon's mouth falls open as the door slams shut. He leaps out of the bin bag.

SIMON *wonderingly* 'My heart's a tall ship and high winds are near.' But what does it mean? How can a heart be a tall ship?' It's the clue. But I don't get it. *Martin Simon walks out of the boys' lavatories, immersed in a book* I know you! You're that ear'ole who passed all those exams and reads poetry! *Martin Simon looks terrified.* Listen, I need your help. You know about this sort of stuff. What does it mean if someone says they're a tall ship?

MARTIN A tall ship?

SIMON That's right. A tall ship.

Martin takes off his spectacles and polishes them nervously.

MARTIN What did this person say exactly?

SIMON *singing loudly* 'Others may –' *He breaks off and eyes the staff-room door warily. Singing softly* 'Others may settle to dandle their babies. My heart's a tall ship, and high winds are near.'

MARTIN Well, obviously, it's a metaphor. The protagonist has chosen to use the analogy of –

Simon seizes *Martin* by the throat.

SIMON   I wasn't asking for a **lecture**. I just want to know what it means.

MARTIN   What it means is that the fellow has to go. Just as a ship with its sails spread has to move with the winds, so this chap knows the moment is coming when, however much he may want to stay, the sort of person he is – the sort of character and temperament he has – will force him to leave. He has no choice.

Simon stares upwards, fighting tears.

SIMON   No choice?

MARTIN   *firmly*   None at all. That's just the way it has to be with someone like him.

SIMON   How can you be so sure?

MARTIN   It's in the words. That's what they mean.

SIMON   But how do you know?

MARTIN   *waving his book*   Listen, you're good with footballs. And I'm good with words.

SIMON   You're right. Well, thanks very much. You've been very helpful. Told me something I really needed to know. Made a big difference.

On an impulse, **Simon** *sticks out a hand.* **Martin** *shakes it.*

MARTIN   Not at all. Any time.

SIMON   No. That's it, I expect. I'm pretty sure I'll be all right now.

Martin leaves. *Simon* sinks in his nest and pulls out his flour baby.

SIMON   I think I will, too. I mean, if that cleverdick ear'ole's right, maybe my dad did even love me, in his way. Mum said he was good with me, while he lasted. In fact, when she caught me cuddling you one evening, she said I reminded her of someone. And she meant him. Well, he's the loser. He's the one who's missed out. Because I reckon babies are the only things on the planet you can love and love, and not get cheesed off with, because they're not pulling their weight in some way. They're not like everyone else. Mum, always telling me to put my plate in the sink, or take my shoes off the sofa. Gran, going on and on about how much I've grown. Sue, teasing me. I used to think people went round saying 'Aah!' to babies as a bit of an act, to cheer up the new parents. But, now I know you, I know different. Babies are **brilliant** things to love. And he missed out on all that. His loss, not mine. And he's missed everything since. Never seen me play football. Never heard me tell a joke. He's just had to get on without me. He's probably got on well enough. But, then again, so have I. And now he's just one of the millions of people on the planet who don't know me. And only the people who know you really count. *Simon jumps out of his bin bag nest.* I feel much better now. I didn't know how much this whole business has been bothering me. But I feel different. *Loudly* I feel **free**!

He leans down to speak to the flour baby sitting in the nest.
Miss Arnott opens the staff-room door.

SIMON You do see, don't you? You do understand?

MR KING *off stage* Who is it?

MISS ARNOTT *dismissively* It's just that crackpot Simon Martin, having a nice little chat with his lump of flour.

MR KING *appearing* Don't knock it. If keeping something safe and close is anything to go by, he'll make a better father than most.

They go back in and shut the door. Light dawns on Simon's face. He holds his flour baby away from him as if she were suddenly infectious.

SIMON She's right. I'm cracked. I'm totally unhinged. *Pause* No, I'm not. I'm finished, that's what I am. Finished. It's all over, that's all. While we were doing it, I made a better father than most. Mr King just said so. I heard him. And maybe one day I will again. One day. Not now. Not even soon. But right now, I'm rescued. I am free again! *He hurls the flour baby in the air and catches her.* Time enough later! When I'm older. When I'm ready. When I don't mind. When the right moment comes. But not now. Oh, no! I'm not going to make the same mistake as my father, and pin myself down years too soon. I'm not going to have to choose between living my life and being in someone else's! *He lifts the flour baby. The bell rings.*

Someone like you. But you're not real. I really did care about you. But you're not real. And I'm not trapped. I have a week of detentions. But they can give me detentions till hell freezes! I'm not **trapped**. *Simon hurls the flour baby in the air. She catches on the light fitting and explodes. Flour showers everywhere. He roots in the bin bag for one flour bag after another, booting them up at the light fitting, where they snag and explode.* Not while I'm *Boot* young, and *Boot* strong, and *Boot* energetic and I can do *Boot* anything, and go *Boot* anywhere! Not while my heart's a tall ship! *Boot* Not while high winds are near!

The staff-room door has opened. **Mr King** *and* **Miss Arnott** *are watching, open-mouthed.* **Rick** *and* **Gwynn** *charge on stage aggressively, skid to a halt, and stand staring. The rest run up behind.* **Mr Cartright** *strides on, clearly ready to speak sharply to* **Simon** *about loitering. He, too, stops and watches.* **Martin Simon** *appears on the other side, immersed in his book. He notices flour raining on the page, and looks up, astonished.* **Dr Feltham** *arrives with a retinue of students.*

SIMON   *singing uproariously*
    'Unfurl the sail, lads, and let the winds find me
    Breasting the soft, sunny, blue rising main –'

Over and over, **Simon** *reaches for handfuls of flour and hurls them round him in a storm*
    'Toss all my burdens and woes clear behind me
    Vow I'll not carry those cargoes again.'

Everyone watches, mesmerized and awestruck, as **Simon** *stands, arms outstretched, a dazzling pillar of pure white in a glorious explosion of flour.*
    'Sail for a sunrise that burns with new maybes.
    Farewell my loved ones, and be of good cheer.'

Everyone stands back respectfully to let him pass as he strides out, singing at the top of his voice.
    'Others may settle to dandle their babies
    My heart's a tall ship, and high winds are near.'

STAGING THE PLAY

The play takes place mainly in Simon Martin's school. Two main areas are needed; the schoolroom and corridor. One scene also takes place in Simon's kitchen.

Think about how you could divide up the performance area to give you these different spaces. Could you use rostra to create different levels? If you have a limited area, how could you create the class-room in such a way that it could be cleared away so you had room for the other scenes? One solution may be to put the classroom onto a truck (a rostrum on wheels) so that it could be wheeled away when not in use.

The door to the staff room is being continually opened and shut, particularly by Miss Arnott in the Third Act. This could be done by building a door and frame into a 'flat'. The flat could be painted to represent the wall of the corridor. If resources stretch far enough, the flat could extend the length of the upstage area with several workable doors through which Dr Feltham and Miss Arnott can burst. The kitchen area also needs a window through which Simon talks to Hyacinth. However, this need not necessarily be a working window.

Suggested set

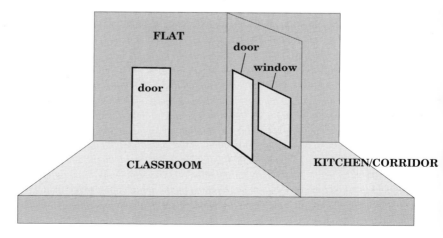

FLAT

door

door

window

CLASSROOM   KITCHEN/CORRIDOR

Sound Effects

See if there are points when sound can be used to highlight the action for comic or dramatic effect, for example, *Baby Love* by The Supremes or *Born to Breed* by Monie Love.

Other times music can be used could be when the other boys taunt Simon by crooning lullabies at him. Compile a list of all the lullabies you know and maybe select one that can be used variously throughout the play.

You could write alternative music for the song "Unfurl the Sail, Lads, and Let the Winds Find Me". Maybe your music teacher could help you do this. The music could then be recorded to be used as a theme or refrain during Simon's monologues or to signal a change of mood.

Anne Fine's original manuscript of the music to 'Unfurl the Sail...'

There are several moments when the classroom is meant to be extremely noisy. When developing the characters it might be a good idea to select a 'sound' that relates to each member of the cast, eg Robin Foster might always be making machine gun sounds. Experiment with this idea and build up a sound that is almost orchestral in effect.

Lighting

Lighting can be used effectively to highlight the different playing areas; think about how the lighting could change to suggest the different moods of the scenes such as using a couple of profile spots or a follow-spot on a largely darkened stage for Simon's monologues.

Costumes

Costumes can be very straightforward as they are mainly school uniform.

Dr Feltham's costume could be quite extreme, in the style of a 'Nutty Professor', with lab coat and dozens of biros in his top pocket.

Make-up

Make-up should be kept simple. The actors playing teachers and Simon's mum could be aged up using costume and movement, rather than unconvincing make-up. Miss Arnott could have an increasingly wild and unkempt hairstyle to reflect her growing instability.

Props

The flour babies are vital props. Read the playwright's description of these carefully and design each 'baby' on paper before making it. The various pieces of scientific equipment that Dr Feltham carries around could be made to look very bizarre in order to highlight the comedy of his scenes.

WORK ON AND AROUND THE SCRIPT

Taking control

At the start of the play, Mr Cartwright is surprised at how easy it is to control the class. How easy is it to get attention and concentration from a group of people? Try the following exercise as a warm-up to the rest of the drama work:

Two people start a scene. When the teacher claps his/her hands, another person walks into the scene and changes it completely. Introduce new people who change the scene until the entire group is involved.

Character Profiles

So that each member of the cast is distinctive in terms of their character, it would be useful to draw up a profile of each character, drawing on information contained in the script and what comes out of your improvisations around the script, that answers the following categories:

Likes:
Dislikes:
Most Annoying Habit:
Most Overused Phrase:

You can extend these categories to include character traits that emerge from your work.

Movement

Think about ways to convey information about your character through movement.

As a group, try these movement exercises:

1) Move around the room as normal; walk at an ordinary pace, then slow down, slow even further down, notice what happens to your shoulders, how you place your feet. Now speed back up to normal pace. Increase your rate of walking, and again until you are almost – but not quite – running. Again come back to a normal pace. Analyze what happens to the position of your body, the angle of your head, the height at which you move, etc.

2) Try the above exercises but this time in your character.

3) Once you feel secure in the work you've done on your character's walk, then extend it to try sitting down and getting up, picking things up, moving objects. It may help to make notes about what you discover.

4) In twos, show each other what you've done. Help each other with positive suggestions about what could be changed or improved.

Drama Work

Some of the characters are very lightly drawn. In order for the performers to make them 'real', it is necessary to build up a past for the characters that explains why they are the way they are at the time of the play.

Work on Mum

Organization: In pairs. One is Mum, one is her friend, Sue.

Situation: Mum is telling Sue that her husband hasn't come back from the shops.

First Line: **MUM**: Where can he be? He's been gone over two hours.

Work on Simon

Organization: In pairs. One of you is Wayne Driscoll and the other is Simon Martin.

Situation: Simon is trying to find out what it would be like to have a dad around.

First Line: **WAYNE**: Sometimes you wish they weren't around. My dad can be a right pain sometimes.

Written Work

Write three separate letters to Simon's dad as if you were Simon. One from when he was about ten years old, one as he would write it at the start of the play, and one as if written at the end of the play.

Draw a diagram showing Simon Martin at the centre of the picture. Now place the name of each character in the play around Simon, showing by how near or far they are to him how important or relevant they are to his life. Remember to include his father and the flour baby. Draw two diagrams, one that shows Simon's relationships at the start of the play and another for the end of the play.

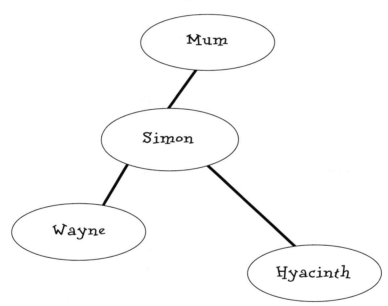

Work on the dialogue

This play was written with a particular group of young people in mind, with a particular social and racial mix.

If you were able to re-write certain bits of the play which words or phrases would you alter and why?

The writer deliberately invented the slang used so that the piece wouldn't date. Look at Act One, scene 2 and try to re-write the scene in language that you and your contemporaries use. You must not lose any information or alter any of the interactions that the scene contains.

Work on Gender

This play was written for a largely male cast. Could you re-write it for a female cast? What would change? Consider the language, the characters, the situations. Look at Simon's scene with his mother (Act II, Scene 1). Try to improvise the scene using two female performers.

Go from...

First Line: **SIMONE**: What was I like at her age, Mum?

Try and get through the scene using whatever dialogue you like. Use whatever information is contained in the scene or invent your own. What changes and why?

Extension

In pairs, improvise the above scene, with a male playing a 'father' and a female playing a Simon-type character. This time the situation is that Mum has left and dad has brought up his daughter on his own. After the improvisation, notice what has changed and what has remained the same in terms of language, emotions and character development.

Group work

For a largely female cast consider how you would tackle Act I, scene 2. Would it be more effective to have a female teacher? How would you make the characters believable as girls?

Drama

1. The Neighbours

Organization: Work in groups of threes or fours. You are neighbours of the Martin family.

Situation: One of you has just seen Simon coming out of the house with his flour baby.

Opening Line: **NEIGHBOUR #1**: What has that terrible boy got there? Is it his football kit?

2. Hyacinth and Simon

Organization: In twos. One is Hyacinth and the other is Simon.

Situation: Hyacinth has seen Simon talking to the flour baby and is very curious.

Opening Line: **HYACINTH**: What's that, Simon? Is it a doll? Can I see?

3. Tableaux.

Organization: In groups representing the Martin family. Show three 'snapshots' of the family: the first when Simon was a baby and the father was there, the second of him leaving, and decide what the third one should be.

4. Cartoons.

Look at the opening scene of the play and develop in small groups a series of cartoon tableaux showing us the 'think' bubbles of the different people involved, eg., Martin Simon's thoughts on entering the classroom. Have the actors speak the lines but get other people not actually in the scene to speak their thoughts. What effect does this have? What other scenes could you do this for, and why?

Writing

1. TV Trailer

Imagine the play is to be shown on television. Using the existing cast, select bits of scenes that can convey a flavour of the play. Write a linking narrative. The trailer should be no longer than sixty seconds.

2. The Review

After reading the play in the classroom or doing a production, write a review of the play as if it is to appear in a national newspaper.

3. The Debate

In a small group in front of the class, take the roles of Interviewer, arts correspondent and playwright and discuss the play as if it was on a TV arts programme.

Comedy

There are many comic moments in the play, especially to do with visual humour. Think about how you can emphasize this, especially in the way that the boys – and teachers – relate to the flour babies. They should almost begin to take on a life of their own. Also look at the way that the prams and the strange pieces of scientific equipment can be exaggerated, not just in the way that the props are made – size, shape, colour – but also how the actors handle them to make them funnier.

Gregory's Girl

ANN   Oh God, not pastry. I hate pastry and it hates me. Give me a ghoulash anyday. It doesn't fight back.

CAROL   She scored three times with him in goal.

SUSAN   Poor Phil.

LIZ   Have you seen his moustache?

CAROL   Anyway he's got to pick her now.

LIZ   Men's hair fascinates me. It's so temporary.

ANN   Equal parts of Trex and lard. Isn't that it?

[*The boys are coming in for the lesson. It is a mixed lesson.* STEVE *is in first. He is a professional. Already he has his bench organised.*]

STEVE   Anyone seen Gregory? He's meant to be working with me . . . oh dear Lizzie, not the hands. Lay off the hands till the last possible minute.

[GREGORY *is late and makes his way through the girls. He is trying to be both charming and surreptitious.*]

GREGORY   Sorry I'm late.

STEVE   Where've you been?

GREGORY   Football.

STEVE   Playing?

GREGORY   No . . . watching. From afar.

STEVE   Hands!

[GREGORY *shows him his hands. It is a routine inspection.*]

GREGORY   That's just paint there.

STEVE   I've got the biscuit mix started, you get on with the sponge and put the oven on, four hundred and fifty degrees.

GREGORY   Yes, boss.

[*Susan approaches* STEVE. *She is wearing a worried look and a grotty apron.*]

SUSAN   Steve, can you help me out with the pastry
             mix thing?
GREGORY   Hello, Susan.

[GREGORY *is ignored.*]

STEVE   Pastry? what pastry? There's more than one
             kind you know. Is it rough puff, short crust
             . . . flaky . . . suet . . . ?

[SUSAN'S *face is a blank.*]

Just tell me, what are you making?

SUSAN   A meat pie. Margaret's doing the Strudel
             Soup, and I'm doing the pie. It's the eggs
             for the pastry that I'm not sure of . . .
STEVE   Strudel soup, eh? I'd like to try some of
             that. It's NOODLE soup , and what eggs?
             You don't put eggs in a pastry. It's 8 ounces
             flour, 4 ounces margarine . . .
GREGORY   . . . a pinch of salt. . .
STEVE   . . . some salt, mix it up, into the oven,
             fifteen minutes . . . and that's it, okay? No
             eggs, no strudels, nothing.
SUSAN   Is that all? That's *simple*, really easy. [*She
             wanders off.*]
STEVE   To think there are five guys in fifth year
             crying themselves to sleep over that.
GREGORY   Six, if you count the music teacher.
STEVE   Watch your mixing, it goes stiff if you
             overdo it, thirty seconds is enough. Give
             me the sugar.
Gregory   It's time *you* were in love. Take your mind
             off all this for a while . . .
STEVE   Plenty of time for love. I'm going to be a
             sex maniac first. Start this summer. Get rid

	of my apron and let my hair down, put love potions in my biscuits. Anyway, I want to be rich first, so that I can love something really . . . expensive.
GREGORY	You're daft. You should try it. Love's great.
STEVE	Who told you?
GREGORY	I'm in love. [*He means it. He is abstractedly stirring the sponge mix with his finger.*] I can't eat, I'm awake half the night, when I think about it I feel dizzy. I'm restless . . . it's wonderful.
STEVE	That sounds more like indigestion.
GREGORY	I'm serious.
STEVE	Or maybe you're pregnant, science is making such progress . . . [STEVE *extracts* GREGORY'S *finger from the mixing bowl and starts to wipe it clean.*] Come on, who is it? Is it a mature woman? Did you do anything dirty? Did you wash your hands?
GREGORY	Don't be crude.
STEVE	Come on! Who is it?
GREGORY	You'll just laugh and tell people.
STEVE	Give us a clue.
GREGORY	[*Reluctantly*] It's somebody in the football team.
STEVE	[*Silent for a moment*] Hey, that's really something. Have you mentioned this to anyone else? Listen, it's probably just a phase . . . is it Andy, no, no . . . is it Pete?
GREGORY	Come on! I mean Dorothy, she came into the team last week. She's in 4A . . . she's a wonderful player, she's a girl. She goes around with Carol and Susan, she's got long lovely hair, she always looks really clean and fresh, and she smells mmm . . . lovely. Even if you pass her in the corridor she smells, mmm, gorgeous . . . She's got teeth, lovely teeth, lovely white, white teeth . .

STEVE	Oh, that Dorothy, the hair . . . the smell . . . the teeth . . . that Dorothy.
GREGORY	That's her, that's Dorothy.
STEVE	The one that took your place in the team.
GREGORY	So what. She's a good footballer. She might be a bit light but she's got skill, she's some girl . . .
STEVE	Can she cook? Can she do this?

[STEVE *throws the rolled out pastry into the air and juggles with a pizza-maker's flourish.*]

GREGORY	[*Being very serious*] When you're in love, things like that don't matter.
STEVE	Gimme the margarine.
GREGORY	Do you think she'll love me back?
STEVE	No chance . . . watch that mix! I told you, nice and slowly . . . take it easy . . . [STEVE takes GREGORY hands in his and guides him through the movements of a nice and easy stir.]
GREGORY	What do you mean no chance?
STEVE	No chance.

From *Gregory's Girl* by Bill Forsyth

In threes, read the above extract. On person plays Steve, one person plays Gregory and one person is the director.
What sort of person is Gregory? What sort of person is Steve? What do learn about them? How do you think they would move? Remember, the scene is set in a crowded domestic science lab.

Drama

The director and performers should answer the above questions and run through the scene. Where are the comic highlights? Agree on these and work out how to maximize them.

THEMES IN AND
AROUND THE PLAY

FAMILIES

Discussion

Simon comes from a one-parent family. Are you or anyone you know from a one-parent family? Divide up into one-parent or two-parent household groups. Each draw up two lists.

List One:

Words or phrases about one-parent families, depending on what group you are in, either from your own experience or what you imagine the experience to be like.

List Two:

Words or phrases about two-parent families. Again, from your own experience or from your ideas or impressions about this type of household.

Share your lists with the whole group. Are there any similarities? Are there different positive and negative aspects about either type of household.

Writing

Collect some information about one-parent families from newspapers and magazines. You could also look at TV programmes, documentaries and sitcoms to get ideas about image.

1) What is the popular image of one-parent families?
2) How is this presented?
3) What is the Government's attitude to one-parent families?
4) What particular problems do one-parent families face?

5) What effect do you think these problems have on:
   a. The children.
   b. The parent.
   c. Society.
6) What help do they have at present to solve these problems?
7) What solutions would you suggest to these problems and issues?

In small groups, divide the work up by taking one question per group and present your findings to the rest of the group. You may want to extend the work by conducting a debate about the study.

Are there any conclusions that can be drawn from the findings? How accurate are the images and information presented to us by the media?

Look at the lists you drew up earlier and see if there is opinion you would now alter in the light of your work.

Contact the National Council for One-Parent Families (address at the back of the book) for further information.

Drama

Organization: In pairs, one is the child, one the parent.
The Situation: The mother has an important job, the child feels neglected.
Opening Line: **MUM**: Come on, hurry up. You're still not ready and I'll be late for work.

Family Planning

ROY: Accident! How horrible! One slip, and your whole life ruined!

In the play, the boys come to realise the enormous responsibility of parenthood. Their response to this is to 'say no'. Apart from saying 'no', what other methods are there of avoiding becoming a father?

Contraception

1. In small groups write down all the stories you have heard about avoiding pregnancy. Share them with the other groups. Do any of them have any basis in reality?

2. In the same groups, write down all the proven methods of contraception with the most effective at the top of the list and the least effective at the bottom.
3. Again, share your lists with the rest of the group to compile a 'master' list. Get in touch with the agencies at the back of this section and see how accurate you were.

Parenting Skills

Are parenting skills taught in your school? If not, do you think you should be taught how to be a good parent and care for small children? What makes a good parent? How could you teach this subject? What aspects of parenting should it cover? How would you teach young people about childcare? On your own or in small groups, put together a scheme of work outlining the subjects that should be covered. Share your scheme with the rest of the group.

CHILD ABUSE

The boys talk about the strains of caring for both flour and real babies. Do you think stress causes abuse? Is it any excuse? What constitutes physical and emotional abuse? Being left to cry all night? Being abandoned, like Simon, by one parent? What signs would you look for that a child was being abused? How would you approach that child? How would you deal with the parents?

Drama

Organization: Two neighbours.
Situation: They are discussing a family in the same road.
Opening Line: **NEIGHBOUR # 1**: You know, I heard that poor kid, Joe, crying late last night. And I could hear shouting and noises. It was terrible.

Organization: In threes. A policeman, a neighbour, a parent.
Situation: The neighbour has heard a child crying in great distress. They have called the police who are now interviewing the parent.
Opening Line: **PARENT**: (To the neighbour) Who asked you to stick your nose in anyway?

Organization: In fours. A social worker, the parents, the child.

Situation: The social worker has been called in to interview parents and child. You may wish to split this into two separate scenes: interview with parents and then with the child.

Opening Line: **SOCIAL WORKER** : I'm sure that if you can talk to me openly we can solve whatever problems there may be.

Read the following extract which is taken from a play about a group of young men who torment a baby. What happens? What is the playwright trying to achieve? Why do you think the young men are so violent towards the baby? What triggers their behaviour? Is it in any way believable? If not, why did the playwright create this scene?

PETE *pulls the pram from* COLIN, *spins it round and pushes it violently at* BARRY. BARRY *sidesteps and catches it by the handle as it goes past.*

BARRY.   Oi...oi!

He looks in the pram.

COLIN.   Wass up?

COLIN *and* PETE *come over*

BARRY.	Yer woke it up.
PETE.	Look at its fists.
COLIN.	Yeh.
PETE.	It's tryin' a clout 'im.
COLIN.	Don't blame it.
PETE.	Goin' a be a boxer.
BARRY.	Is it a girl?
PETE.	Yer wouldn't know the difference.
BARRY.	'Ow d'yer get 'em t'sleep?
PETE.	Pull their 'air.
COLIN.	Eh?
PETE.	Like that.

He pulls his hair.

COLIN.   That 'urt.

They laugh.

```
MIKE.      Wass 'e doin'?
COLIN.     Pullin' its 'air.
FRED.      'E'll 'ave its ol' woman after 'im.
MIKE.      Poor sod.
BARRY.     'E's showin' off.
COLIN.     'E wants the coroner's medal.
MIKE (comes to the pram). Less see yer do it.
```

PETE *pulls its hair.*

```
           O yeh.
BARRY.     It don't say nothin'.
COLIN.     Little bleeder's 'alf dead a fright.
MIKE.      Still awake.
PETE.      Ain' co-operatin'.
BARRY.     Try a pinch.
MIKE.      That ought a work.
BARRY.     Like this.
```

He pinches the baby.

```
COLIN.     Look at that mouth.
BARRY.     Flippin' yawn.
PETE.      Least it's tryin'.
MIKE.      Pull its drawers off.
COLIN.     Yeh!
MIKE.      Less case its ol' crutch.
PETE.      Ha!
BARRY.     Yeh!
```

He throws the nappy in the air.

```
           Yippee!
COLIN.     Look at that!
```

They laugh.

```
MIKE.      Look at its little legs goin'.
COLIN.     Ain' they ugly!
BARRY.     Ugh!
MIKE.      Can't keep 'em still!
PETE.      'Avin a fit.
BARRY.     It's dirty.
```

They groan.

```
COLIN.     'Old its nose.
MIKE       Thass for 'iccups.
BARRY.     Gob its crutch.
```

> *He spits.*
>
> MIKE.   Yeh!
> COLIN.   Ha!
> MIKE.   Got it!
> PETE.   Give it a punch.
> MIKE.   Yeh less!
> COLIN.   There's no-one about!
>
> PETE *punches it*
>
> Ugh! Mind yer don't hurt it.
> MIKE.   Yer can't.
> BARRY.   Not at that age.
> MIKE.   Course yer can't, no feelin's.
> PETE.   Like animals.
> MIKE.   'It it again.
> COLIN.   I can't see!
> BARRY.   'Arder.
> PETE.   Yeh.
> BARRY.   Like that.
>
> *He hits it.*
>
> From *Saved* by Edward Bond

In small groups, cast and rehearse this scene. Think carefully about the blocking, ie., where, when, how and why the actors move in relation to each other and to the pram. Consider how to build the horror of the piece. Improvise the scene immediately beforehand between the mother, Pam and the father, Fred, and use this to work out how to bring on the other members of the gang and flow into the scene you have just worked on.

1. Before
Organization: In pairs, one is the mother, Pam and the other is the father, Fred.
Situation: Pam needs to leave the baby for a short period.
Opening Line: **PAM**: For crying out loud, Fred. Can't you look after him for just five minutes?

2. The Mother
Organization: The playwright didn't write a scene where the mother discovers the death of the baby. Improvise the scene and maybe add it onto to the end of the scripted scene you have already worked on.

Situation: Either individually or in pairs with one as director.

Opening Line: **PAM**: Have you bin a good boy while I've bin away? (looks into pram) Whasser matter wiv you? Oh my God!

3. The Courtroom Scene

Organization: Two or three members of the gang. Clerk of the Court. Judge. Witnesses.

Situation: The gang members are on trial for the murder of the baby. Decide who else should be in the scene. Maybe there was a witness to the crime. Maybe character witnesses will appear for the lads. Set up the room as much like a court as possible.

Opening Line: **CLERK OF THE COURT**: You are hereby charged with the murder of John Stevens. How do you plead?

SCHOOL FOR PARENTS

Simon has very little actual information about his father. He may well invest him with qualities that he does not possess. Is this a common problem when people think about absent parents?

Drama

Organization: In groups of four; one is the child or young person, the other three are prospective 'parents' (depending on the genders, they are either 'mothers' or 'fathers'). The teacher should secretly give each 'parent' a characteristic such as impatience, selfishness, childishness, or whatever.

Situation: The 'child' has to interview each 'parent' as to their suitability to care for them and select the best candidate.

Extension: The same situation but the characteristics are much more ambiguous, for example, over-imaginative, over-protective, selfless, etc.

Writing

On your own or in small groups , write a "Wanted" poster for ideal parents, maybe separating out mothers and fathers and listing or drawing up a profile of distinguishing positive qualities and skills.

FUTURE PARENTS

Organization: Working as a whole group, divide into pairs: mother and father. The teacher could take the role of Controller.

Situation: It is some time in the future when only carefully selected couples are allowed to become parents. They have to apply to the authorities for permission to have children. With your partner, think carefully about the qualities that you each possess and how these will determine whether you will be chosen to become parents.

Opening Line: **CONTROLLER**: (To first couple) Approach and present your case.

ETHICS AND PARENTHOOD

Task

Collect newspaper reports about current issues like multiple births and selective termination. How do the different media (i.e. TV, tabloid and 'quality' newspapers) approach these topics? Compile a TV programme reporting on these issues. Consider how you would present the Law's view, the Government's guidelines, the families involved. Role-play the different spokespeople and decide whether your programme will have a particular bias towards one view or another or if it will be purely factual and objective.

Fathers

The author of the play is making a point about people having to be ready before they have babies. Do you think that men and women are different in this respect? If so, in what way? Can a young father be as responsible and nurturing as a young mother? Think about how fathers are presented in the media. For example, *Three Men and a Baby* was a comic film about how inexperienced men coped with looking after a new-born baby. What made the film funny? Could you use any of the ideas from the film, e.g. the difficulties of putting on a nappy, in your production of *Flour Babies*?

Read the following extract.

Fergal Keane, BBC foreign correspondent, writes a letter to his new-born son, Daniel.

My Dear Son...

It is six o'clock in the morning on the island of Hong Kong. You are asleep, cradled in my left hand and I am learning the art of one-handed typing. Your mother, more tired yet more happy than I have ever known her, is sound asleep in the room next door and there is a soft quiet in our apartment. Since your arrival, days have melted into night and back again and we are learning a new grammar – a long sentence whose punctuation marks are feeding and winding and nappy-changing and those occasional moments of quiet...

Your coming has turned me upside down and inside out. So much that seemed essential to me has, in the past few days, taken on a different colour. Like many foreign corespondents I know, I have lived a life that on occasion has veered along the edge – war zones, natural disasters, darkness in all its shapes and forms. In a world of insecurity and ambition and ego, it is easy to be drawn in, to take chances with our lives, to believe what we do, and what people say about us, is reason enough to gamble with death. Now, looking at your sleeping face inches away from me, listening to your occasional sigh and gurgle, I wonder how I could ever have thought glory and prizes and praise were sweeter than life.

It is also true that I am pained - perhaps haunted is a better word – by the memory, suddenly so vivid now, of each suffering child I have come across on my journeys. To tell the truth, it is almost too much to bear at this moment to even think of children being hurt and abused and killed. And yet, looking at you, the images come flooding back. Ten-year-old Ande Mikail dying from napalm burns on a hillside in Eritrea. How his voice cried out, growing ever more faint, when the wind blew dust into his wounds; the two brothers Domingo and Juste in Menongue, Southern Angola – Juste three years old, blind and dying from malnutrition, being carried on ten-year-old Domingo's back, and Domingo's words to me: 'He was so nice before, but now he has the hunger.' The hunger. The loss. The total end of innocence.

...I have looked into the eyes of children and have turned away because I have seen the promise of life ravaged by loss. I have seen what happens when adults give them knives and guns and drugs. Little boys are capable of terrible acts, Daniel, terrible imitations of the adult world.

From *My Dear Son* by Fergal Keane

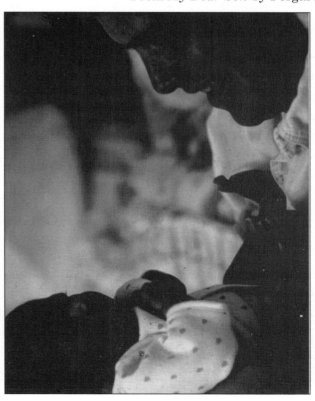

Is this piece of writing moving? Is it 'soppy'? If so, why? Do you think the fact that the author is the father rather than the mother affects the way he writes? Does a father have different hopes and fears for his young son?

Writing

Imagine you are the mother or father of a new-born baby. Write a short letter to them, maybe taking up some of the ideas that Fergal Keane has used as a starting point. Decide what your personal hopes and fears are for the child and what you can promise it through its life.

Fathers and babies are now popular subjects for posters.

The Child

How can I teach, how can I save,
This child whose features are my own,
Whose feet run down the ways where I have walked?

How can I name that vision past the corner,
How warn the seed that grows to constant anger,
How can I draw the map that tells no lies?

His world is a small world of hours and minutes,
Hedgerows shut in the horizons of his thought,
His loves are uncritical and deep,
His anger innocent and sudden like a minnow.

His eyes, acute and quick, are unprotected,
Unsandalled still, his feet run down the lane,
Down to that lingering horror in the brambles,
The limp crashed airman, in the splintered goggles.

c.1939 Michael Roberts

Read the above poem. How does the writer convey the child's view of the world? What does the 'father' in the poem want to warn or tell his son about? Do you think the boy actually sees an airman or is it a metaphor? If so, for what? Is it significant that the poem was written in 1939?

Drama

In groups, divide into two smaller groups. One group should work out how to say the poem and one group could stage tableaux to illustrate it. Try different ways of dividing up the lines to make the most of the rhythms. Also make your tableaux clear and work out a way to move slowly and non-distractingly from one image to another.

Extension: Try and put both groups together so you are all performing both the words and the movements. Think about other sounds you could blend in, for example, ticking clocks for the line "His world is a small world of hours and minutes."

75

Child Care in Nottingham

The procedure we adopted was to ask the mothers whether the fathers took an active part in doing things for the children: specifically, we asked whether the father would give the baby his food, change his nappy, give him a bath, get him to sleep, attend to him in the night, take him out without his mother, and play with him. The answers to these questions also had to be qualified according to whether he undertook each activity often, sometimes, or not at all.

Not unexpectedly, we found that some of the activities of child care were more popular than others with the fathers (see Table). Whereas 80 per cent were prepared to get the baby to sleep, for instance, only 57 per cent ever changed a nappy, and still fewer (39 per cent) ever gave him his bath.

The total of 68 per cent who, at least sometimes, take the baby out without the mother is perhaps surprising in view of the traditional reluctance of the Englishman to be seen pushing a pram; and this percentage does not include fathers who "wouldn't mind doing it, but we always go out as a family". Many fathers took all the young children out of the mother's way on a Saturday or Sunday morning, while she cleared up; and a large number, especially those living on new housing estates, regularly took the baby without its mother on a visit to the paternal grandmother in the older part of the city. One father, who lived on the new council estate outside the city, cycled the seven miles to his mother's terrace house every Saturday afternoon with the baby sitting on the cross-bar.

Table showing proportions of fathers undertaking various activities in the care of one-year-olds

	Feed baby	Change nappy	Play with baby	Bath baby	Get to sleep	Attend in the night	Take out alone
	%	%	%	%	%	%	%
Often	34	20	83	15	31	18	29
Sometimes	44	37	16	24	49	32	39
Never	22	43	1	61	20	50	32

Statistics

Read the extract on page 76. These figures were collected in 1980. Do you think anything has changed in the nineties?

Task

Conduct a survey amongst your own friends and family who have babies under the age of one year. Analyze your findings in the same way as the table on page 76.

To calculate percentages, divide the smaller figure by the larger and then multiply by one hundred. For example, "4 out of 7 fathers often feed the baby" can be calculated as follows:

$4 \div 7 \times 100 = 57\%$ (rounded down to the nearest whole number).

Soap operas

Think about some examples of fathers from soap operas, particularly those who have been re-united with children they left or abandoned earlier. For example, David Wicks in *EastEnders* and his children Bianca and Joe. How did he handle getting to know his children again? How did the mothers respond? What did the children want from him? Was David a good father?

LITERATURE

Read the following extract taken from Mary Shelley's gothic horror story, *Frankenstein*.

I T WAS ON A DREARY NIGHT of November that I beheld the accomplishment of my toils. With an anxiety that almost amounted to agony, I collected the instruments of life around me, that I might infuse a spark of being into the lifeless thing that lay at my feet. It was already one in the morning; the rain pattered dismally against the panes, and my candle was nearly burnt out, when, by the glimmer of the half-extinguished light, I saw the dull yellow eye of the creature open; it breathed hard, and a convulsive motion agitated its limbs.

How can I describe my emotions at this catastrophe, or how delineate the wretch whom with such infinite pains and care I had endeavoured to form? His limbs were in proportion, and I had selected his features as beautiful. Beautiful! - Great God! His yellow skin scarcely covered the work of muscles and arteries underneath; his hair was of a lustrous black, and flowing; his teeth of a pearly whiteness; but these luxuriances only formed a more horrid contrast with his watery eyes, that seemed almost of the same colour as the dun white sockets in which they were set, his shrivelled complexion and straight black lips.

The different accidents of life are not so changeable as the feelings of human nature. I had worked hard for nearly two years, for the sole purpose of infusing life into an inanimate body. For this I had deprived myself of rest and health. I had desired it with an ardour that far exceeded moderation; but now that I had finished, the beauty of the dream vanished, and breathless horror and disgust filled my heart. Unable to endure the aspect of the being I had created, I rushed out of the room, and

continued a long time traversing my bedchamber, unable to compose my mind to sleep. At length lassitude succeeded to the tumult I had before endured; and I threw myself on the bed in my clothes, endeavouring to seek a moment of forgetfulness.

But it was in vain: I slept, indeed, but I was disturbed by the wildest dreams. I thought I saw Elizabeth, in the bloom of health, walking in the streets of Ingolstadt. Delighted and surprised, I embraced her; but as I imprinted the first kiss on her lips, they became livid with the hue of death; her features appeared to change, and I thought that I held the corpse of my dead mother in my arms; a shroud enveloped her form, and I saw grave-worms crawling in the folds of the flannel.

I started from my sleep with horror; a cold dew covered my forehead, my teeth chattered, and every limb became convulsed: when, by the dim and yellow light of the moon, as it forced its way through the window shutters, I beheld the wretch – the miserable monster whom I had created. He held up the curtain of the bed: and his eyes, if eyes they may be called, were fixed on me. His jaws opened, and he muttered some inarticulate sounds, while a grin wrinkled his cheeks. He might have spoken, but I did not hear; one hand was stretched out, seemingly to detain me, but I escaped, and rushed down stairs. I took refuge in the courtyard belonging to the house which I inhabited; where I remained for the rest of the night, walking up and down in the greatest agitation, listening attentively, catching and fearing each sound as if it were to announce the approach of the demoniacal corpse to which I had so miserably given life.

Oh! no mortal could support the horror of that countenance. A mummy again endued with animation could not be so hideous as that wretch. I had gazed on him while unfinished; he was ugly then; but when those muscles and joints were rendered capable of motion, it became a thing such as even Dante could not have conceived.

I passed the night wretchedly. Sometimes my pulse beat so quickly and hardly that I felt the palpitation of every artery; at others I nearly sank to the ground through languor and extreme weakness. Mingled with this horror, I felt the bitterness of disappointment; dreams that had been my food and pleasant rest for so long a space were now become a hell to me; and the change was so rapid, the overthrow so complete!

From *Frankenstein by* Mary Shelley

Frankenstein is about a scientist who creates a monster from the limbs and organs of corpses. Some people think that this is a story about men's envy of women's ability to produce life. How do men usually satisfy this creative urge? If science were able to do it, should men have the right to bear children? Do film comedies like *Junior* (where a man has a baby) look forward to the time when this may be possible?

Writing

Write a poem from the monster's point of view, maybe from the time he realises what he is. Alternatively write a poem as if you are the first man in the world expecting the first man-produced baby.

TV versions

You may have seen versions of the Frankenstein story on television. Re-write this extract as a TV script; remember to include atmospheric lighting and music. Remember, Frankenstein is the name of the creator, not the monster.

FROM NOVEL TO PLAY

Dutifully, Mr Cartright strolled over the room to correct Simon's pitiful spelling. But before reaching down to despoil the last diary entry with his marking pen, he stood quietly behind the desk for a few moments, practising the skilled decoder's art.

Day 18. Over & Out.

So I was all wrong about the Glorious Explosion and getting to kick the flour babies to bits at the end. Who cares? I was planning on cheating anyway. I was going to hide mine, and join in battering everyone else's. I might be in 4C but I'm not absolutely stupid . I worked out days ago that I wouldn't be able to hurt mine, not any more, not now I've grown to like her. (And especially not now, when everyone hates me and I have no fr–

Mr Cartright was just leaning over, pen uncapped, to rearrange the next two vowels, when both of them disappeared before his eyes, dissolving in a miniature blue pool.

A teardrop. No doubt about it. And just like everything else about the boy, it was enormous. Hastily, before more could fall, Mr Cartright dug in his jacket pocket, fished out the huge spotted handkerchief and thrust it into Simon's hand.

Simon stared at the large blue blur on his work. No doubt about it. It was a teardrop. What was the matter with him? If he didn't get a grip, the others might notice. Come break-time, he would be *destroyed*.

Gratefully he took the handkerchief he was offered. And while Mr Cartright heaved his massive back end up on Simon's desk, deliberately shielding him from everyone's view, he tried to pull himself together.

When Mr Cartright felt the damp handkerchief pushed back in his hand, he took it that it was safe to slide off the desk, and carry on reading.

I really liked having that flour baby to look after, even though I got sick of her and she drove me mad. I liked seeing her sitting on top of the wardrobe watching me as I lay in bed at night. I liked chatting to her at breakfast. And I liked cuddling her to make Macpherson jealous. Just last night, when I was rocking her in my arms, Mum said I reminded her of someone. She didn't say who, and I didn't have to ask. But it was good to know he used to rock me like that when I was a baby. Maybe he did really love me, in his way.

Quite forgetting, in the emotion of the moment, that the handkerchief had already been pressed into service more than once, Mr Cartright drew it out, and, lighting on a fairly dry patch, blew his nose in a trumpeting fashion. Then, bravely, he forced himself to read to the end.

He just wasn't very good at showing it, running away like that. But I can't talk, can I? My flour baby ended up such a mess, I practically got my ears torn off. But I really did care about her. I really did.

Mr Cartright could bear it no longer. 'For heaven's sake, lad,' he whispered hoarsely. 'If you love the thing that much, go and fish it out of the waste bin. Take it home.'

Simon said nothing. But, flushing scarlet, he unconsciously leaned forward and gripped the sides of his desk.

Slowly, suspiciously, Mr Cartright tipped Simon back a few inches, lifted the desk lid, and peered in.

The flour baby peered back at him anxiously, out of the dark.

Mr Cartright lowered the desk lid. He looked at Simon. Simon looked at him. Then Mr Cartright said:

'Do you want to know your problem, Simon Martin? You sell yourself too short. Your flour baby is a squalid and disgusting little creature. She wouldn't pass any hygiene tests, and, if she were real, she wouldn't win any Natty Baby competitions. But if keeping what you care for close and safe counts for anything, I'll tell you this. You'll make a better father than most.'

Then, clearing his throat loudly, he strode off as fast as he could, back to the sanctuary of his own desk.

From *Flour Babies* by Anne Fine

Writing

Read the extract on page 82-3 carefully. In twos (or threes, with one as director) either extract dialogue from the play to use or write your own. Play the scene through and consider how to make the most of it, paying particular attention to the pathos and the element of comedy and how to achieve this balance. Why do you think that Anne Fine did not include this scene in the play?

Drama

Now play the scene in threes; Mr Cartwright, Simon and a director (optional).

1) Try playing the scene in different ways; try it with both actors speaking very quietly, what effect does this have? Then try it with one being quiet and the other being loud.
2) Can the scene be directed to a climax? How can this be achieved?
3) Experiment with how close the actors are to each other. What effect does placing Mr Cartwright higher than Simon have? Look at how changing height, distance and focus between the actors alters the impact of the scene.

Read the following extract:

TOO MUCH, TOO YOUNG...

CHRIS EDGE has not had a good year. In January, his wife Clare threw him out of their flat and started divorce proceedings. A couple of months later, her new boyfriend punched Chris in the face and broke his nose, then the boyfriend fractured Chris's jaw. Two weeks later, Chris was sacked from his job. And now he is limbering up for what promises to be a bloody fight for the custody of his 21-month-old daughter, Natasha.

Going through all this in private would have been painful enough, but Chris had had to endure the extra knife-twist of having his troubles recounted by his wife in The News of the World. Millions of people read lines such as: 'It was when I realized that I couldn't stand the sound of Chris eating that I realized we should never have married.' Other papers ran stories about his annoying habits, his untidiness and his alleged heavy drinking.

They are interested not because Chris is famous or rich or powerful. He is none of these things and neither is Clare. They are interested because he is 18-years-old. Clare is younger still. She was 15 when she got pregnant with Natasha and 16 when she married Chris. Now, at 17, she has been granted a divorce.

...Chris Edge met Clare Butler when he was 15 and she was 14. They were at school in Birmingham, studying for their GCSEs. Although Clare's dad had left her mum a year or two earlier, both came from relatively happy, hard-working homes. They were promising pupils. Clare was a talented dancer with ambitions to turn professional. Chris's mum, a child-minder, hoped he might be the first member of the family to go to university.

They didn't sleep together at first – not for nine months until it felt right. Then, when they did, they made sure they were careful, using condoms every time. Yet somehow Clare got pregnant. She had no idea at first, but her mother, Linda, had an instinct. Clare says: 'She looked at me one night when I was doing my maths homework and said, "You're not pregnant, are you?" I just laughed but the next day she took me to the doctor and I tested positive.'

...Far from being nonchalant, the young couple were paralyzed with worry, terrified of what Chris's parents would say when they rang to tell them the news. They were right to be. Over the next few weeks, along with almost every adult they knew, Dennis and Julie Edge tried to persuade Clare to have an abortion.

'Chris's mum said she didn't agree with abortions – as she thought they were disgusting – but I should have one anyway,' Clare recalls.

....If Chris were a proper feckless youth in tabloid mould, he would have run off at this point. Instead, he told Clare that whatever she did, he would stand by her. And when she decided to have the baby, he took the extraordinarily old-fashioned step of asking her to marry him. 'I thought it was the right thing to do,' he says now, 'I hadn't been banking on her getting pregnant because I was only 16, but when she did, I wanted us to be a proper family. She was our baby, wasn't she?'

...When Natasha was born in October 1994, they were thrilled and had the baby christened in church before marrying two months later. Despite still being squashed into the single bed, with the baby's cot taking up most of the rest of Clare's childhood bedroom, they got on well... Chris was working and bringing in money. Clare was back at school taking her GCSEs....

Then, Clare left school, they moved into their own flat, and everything went wrong. It was a nice place, above a newsagent. 'Everything should have been fine, but somehow it just fell apart', Chris says. He blames it on a holiday Clare took in Italy with a friend that summer, where he says she had a brief affair. 'She had a different attitude towards marriage after that and I did not cope with it very well,' he says.

Clare puts it down simply to too much, too young. 'I woke up one day and realized we had done everything and I was only 16. It was boring. Before, every day was different, now it was the same routine. I used to get up, wash the baby, feed the baby. Chris was at work. I would have dinner ready for him when he got home. He would wash up. I would dry up, then I would put the washing on, do the ironing and go to bed. Then we would get up the next day and do it all over again.' Boredom bred contempt. They started to argue, usually over silly things like tidying up and cooking...Eventually, Clare told Chris she wanted a divorce.

From *It Was Just Too Much, Too Young*, Lisa O'Kelly, The Observer 1996

FURTHER WORK

Writing

1. Write an article for your local paper entitled "Teenage Fathers in Britain Today".
2. Think over some of the issues that have come out of your discussions around the play. Make up a magazine advice page and contribute letters about problems to the page. Try and answer the letters with advice and common sense.
3. Prepare a TV programme about teenage fathers in Britain today. What are their biggest problems? What is the image of young parents in the media? Decide how you would put the programme together. Role-play being parents, teenagers, social workers, teachers, health workers and the documentary makers. Draw up interview questions and try and create a balanced view.

FURTHER READING

Dear Nobody by Berlie Doherty, Harper Collins Children's
Books (novel), Collins Educational (playscript).
Teen Scene: Pregnancy by Anne Coates, Wayland.
Flour Babies by Anne Fine, Puffin Books.
Ruth by Elizabeth Gaskell, Wordsworth Classics.

USEFUL AGENCIES

Brook Advisory Centre, 165 Grays Inn Road, WC1.
(0171-713 9000)
National Council For One-Parent Families,
225 Kentish Town Road, NW5. (0171- 267 1361)